'I came to apologise.'

Nick closed the  t it. 'I have no right

'Are you misera
is your big day.' ow

'Is it?'

'It should be,' she insisted quietly. 'Getting engaged is a sort of—of gesture of fidelity, a promise.'

Nick turned to face her, slanting a look of almost scathing amusement at her.

'Maybe I'm not making any such promise.'

'Then you shouldn't be getting engaged… This is just another ploy to put me off my stride tomorrow.'

'How could I?' he asked softly. 'Who could put you off your stride?'

'You could… It doesn't matter,' she said in a whisper. 'I intend to survive.'

'Oh, we'll both survive,' Nick assured her softly, 'so let's say goodnight.'

Victoria turned to look at him. His gaze ran slowly over her face and then he swept her closely into his arms, kissing her startled lips with sudden urgency.

Patricia Wilson was born in Yorkshire and lived there until she married and had four children. She loves travelling and has lived in Singapore, Africa and Spain. She had always wanted to be a writer but a growing family and career as a teacher left her with little time to pursue her interest. With the encouragement of her family she gave up teaching in order to concentrate on writing and her other interests of music and painting.

Recent titles by the same author:

AN INNOCENT CHARADE
BORROWED WIFE
MACBRIDE'S DAUGHTER

COURTING
TROUBLE

BY
PATRICIA WILSON

First published in Great Britain 1997
Harlequin Mills & Boon Limited,
Eton House, 18-24 Paradise Road, Richmond, Surrey TW9 1SR

© Patricia Wilson 1997

ISBN 0 263 80175 6

Set in Times Roman 10½ on 11¼ pt.
02-9707-55876 C1

Printed and bound in Great Britain
by Mackays of Chatham PLC, Chatham

CHAPTER ONE

VICTORIA waited outside Nick's study and tried to judge if the moment was right. Probably not. He had been distant for months. This was ridiculous really, hanging around like a schoolgirl, but she didn't want any trouble with him. She had been too close to him for too long just to shrug and forget all about it. Nevertheless there were some things she just could not face and his engagement was one of them.

The trouble was, as soon as she told him he would explode, or, worse still, turn to ice. She could cope with a battle but she hated his stony silences. She had always adored him, but now he had pushed her right out of his life.

'Come in, Victoria. I can see you lurking about and the suspense is killing me.' The voice came unexpectedly and Victoria found her cheeks flushing with embarrassment. He was always one jump ahead of everyone, especially her, and she knew how that voice could change; she'd heard it in the courtroom plenty of times—one minute a silky-dark sensuous sound and the next minute a tiger's roar.

'I was wondering whether to bother you at the moment. I know you've got the big case and you can't be late and...'

'I always have time for my nearest and dearest.' He turned those dark grey eyes on her. 'Walk into my parlour.'

Victoria knew all about the spider and the fly. She *really* understood it. It came back to her strongly as she stepped inside the study door. She didn't feel like going

5

in further. All the same, she had come to make a declaration. It had to be done and now was as good a time as any.

'What can I do for you?' After inviting her in, Nick's attention returned to his desk. There was an important court case going on and she knew he was terribly busy. Victoria wished she had put this off, but she had been doing that for ages and it had to be said some time.

'Well, actually, it's about your engagement party,' she managed brightly. 'I'm sorry but I can't go. Something came up at the office and—'

'You *will* go, Victoria!'

Nick looked up and stared at her, his eyes stony, dark grey, inflexible. There was no expression on his handsome face now. He didn't even look particularly angry, but then he never did. He had always been in control of his emotions and his unbending attitude infuriated her instantly. Nick had been like this for so long that she had almost forgotten what he used to be like.

'I didn't come in here to ask your permission,' she reminded him sharply. 'Out of common courtesy I came to tell you that I am not going to your engagement party. I have to work too, you know. I have a big presentation that can't be reorganised. I'm not about to lose my job just because of your engagement party. There's not going to be any sort of discussion. I'm just not going.'

'Oh, yes, you are,' he murmured, almost absently.

He went on doing what he had been doing before she came in, collecting papers, sliding them into a briefcase, every action methodical. The only real attention he had paid to her had been that one dark grey stare and the wryly amused look he had given her as she'd stepped in through the door. Now he was ignoring her.

Normally it would have been enough to intimidate her. When Nick's eyes went cold and flat it was like looking into a deep grey sea, bottomless, frightening, but this time Victoria had no intention of losing. The idea of going to a stuffy, formal engagement party made her shudder, and she didn't want to watch Nick getting engaged. She knew it would hurt. She was finally losing him. Work had seemed like a good excuse but, as usual, he was trying to override her.

'Look, this party has nothing to do with me,' she pointed out in exasperation. 'I'm just giving you good warning so that you can tell Cheryl's parents and sort out any seating arrangements—'

'It's a buffet,' he interrupted in the same detached voice. 'A marquee on the lawn with the sides open to take advantage of the good weather and show off the garden. Lots of tulle drapes, flowers on stands—not out of the garden, of course. In the evening there will be a dance—inside.' He didn't look up. The briefcase was snapped shut, one quick glance flashed around his desk, and quite obviously he was preparing to walk out.

Victoria almost gaped at him, her anger momentarily stilled by astonishment. He wasn't paying any attention to her at all. Nothing she had said had been even slightly considered. Moreover, his voice might have been detached but there had also been an almost contemptuous tone to it when he had spoken of the arrangements for his engagement party.

He had painted a swift and pithy picture of a scene that would be photographed by all the society magazines and Victoria almost cringed. If anyone could be twee on a grand scale then Cheryl Ashton's parents would take the prize. It would be pink, white and gold, and the tulle would float in the slight breeze. Any boisterous weather and Lady Ashton would panic and blame everyone around her.

Nick had managed to get all that across with few words. But then, if he couldn't, who could? Victoria had seen him in action in court more than once. He could make even a hardened judge blink with just one sentence. She took a steadying breath. He might be a famous and skilful barrister, but he was not going to intimidate her!

'Very interesting,' she managed ironically, 'but as I'm not going it doesn't really concern me. I'll make a note of the arrangements, though, and add them to my memoirs in about thirty years.'

She turned to walk out of his study, intent on disappearing while she was in the lead, but Nick's voice stopped her.

'My engagement party is two weeks from now. As a member of this family you will attend. You will travel with Mother, Father and Tony and you will not cause any upset or embarrassment.'

'I'm not a member of—'

Victoria's heated rejoinder to this arbitrary order was silenced as Nick's eyes narrowed to a dangerous glitter.

'Don't say it, Victoria,' he warned harshly. 'Caution was never your strong point and when you're angry everything comes out wrongly. Stop while you're ahead because you're stepping on very thin ice.'

'I'm not ahead!' she stormed, flustered by his swift anger at her nearly voiced truth. 'You haven't listened to one thing I've said.'

'I don't miss much,' he growled. 'Now let the matter drop. I'm in court in two hours and it's a hell of a drive to London. I should have stayed in my flat and then I would have missed all this nonsense.'

'All right!' Her brilliantly blue eyes flashed up at him as she turned to leave. 'But as far as I'm concerned you've been warned. Nobody is ordering me about and I've declined the invitation in the proper way.'

'The proper way?' He raised dark brows and regarded her in a cold, sceptical manner. 'You had an engraved invitation.'

'And I replied promptly on headed notepaper!' Victoria said sarcastically. 'I intend to post it off to Cheryl's parents this morning.' She marched to the door but Nick's voice was almost in her ear as she got there.

'Don't!' he warned quietly. 'When you have to change your mind you'll only look foolish and we'll all hate that.'

When she turned to look up at him in annoyance, her eyes opened wider at the speed with which he had moved closer to threaten her. One minute he had been by his desk and now he was towering over her. He could be very unnerving.

She stepped quickly into the deserted hall and gave him one more defiant glance, but his look worried her. He was absolutely adamant about this party and she had never succeeded in getting the better of him—ever.

'I won't be changing my mind.'

'You will. Mother and Father like to show you off. If you don't go they'll have a lot of explaining to do because your absence will look ill-mannered and spiteful. You haven't one good excuse, Victoria, and I doubt if even Tony will be able to cover for you this time. I won't even try. Your place is with Mother and Father at my engagement party. Tony will hold your hand and soothe your temper,' he finished scathingly.

'You're hateful, Nick!' She said it bitterly and he nodded, his eyes still that stony grey, still staring down at her.

'It's the company I keep.' He turned to the front door, his parting shot aimed over his shoulder. 'Did you forget to brush your hair this morning?'

Victoria's hand went defensively to her unruly mane of fair hair, even though she knew she had brushed it vigorously. Before she could recover he was out of the door and stepping into his car, on his way to London and his world of cold, quick wits and power.

She had lost. Deep inside she knew it, because she could not think of one good excuse to miss this awful party. Nick was right; it would hurt Muriel and Frank. Imagining she could get the better of Nick was idiotic too. He was a fierce adversary in court and nowadays his attitude to her was little better.

She went angrily up to her room, uneasy about her appearance after his last remark. Nick had changed the whole atmosphere of this house over the past few years. Clifford Court had been her joy and refuge for over twelve years. Nick had once been her refuge too, but now he was constantly unbending, waiting for her to put a foot wrong and more than ready to snap her head off when she did. To go to his engagement party and smile sweetly at the Ashtons would be more than she could handle.

Cheryl Ashton never had a hair out of place.

Her home was probably the same, and her mother and father had permanent smiles etched on their faces, no doubt to draw attention away from their glassy eyes. She had been to a very stiff dinner party with them in London, when Nick had decided to introduce them to his family, so she knew without doubt what they were like.

Nick's brother, Tony, was enthusiastic about the whole thing, desperately anxious to be Nick's best man, but Victoria was angry, restless and filled with rebellious thoughts. She couldn't even begin to think why Nick was marrying Cheryl Ashton. It had all happened so quickly, and as far as she could see they had nothing in common.

She wasn't even sure why she was fuming about it. Nick would be moving out, into a home of his own, and then the atmosphere at Clifford Court would settle back to normality and the comfortable happiness she was used to. He was away a lot anyway. His workload was tremendous, and more often than not he had to stay in his flat in London so that he would be in court on time. When he came home they argued or he ignored her.

Thank goodness Tony hadn't changed. He was still her amusing friend, her confidant. He still plotted with her as much as he had done when she had first come here and even being a solicitor hadn't changed him. Only Nick had changed.

Victoria stared at herself in the mirror. For wildly curling locks, her hair was extremely neat, actually. Nick's remark had been typical of his attitude to her. Sapphire-blue eyes looked back at her and she realised that they were anything but normal; they were a bit desperate. She looked angry, flushed and not at all in control of herself.

It wouldn't do. She should be quite used to Nick's attitude by now—after all, he had been like this for over three years. It still annoyed her, and sometimes it hurt, but there was no way he would ever find out that last fact. If he wanted a battle she would take him on.

She gathered her things and prepared to go down to breakfast. Nick wasn't the only one who had to get to work. She didn't have to leave at the crack of dawn, but she still had to be in London by nine. He'd used to give her a lift to work, but that was in the past. Victoria frowned. She wouldn't want a lift nowadays anyway. He had hardly ever spoken to her, and he'd used to look at her warningly as he dropped her off at work, as if she was about to do something dreadful.

'I hate you, Nick King,' she announced loudly to her reflection in the mirror.

It wasn't true but it made her feel slightly clever, as if she had got the better of him, and she hoped her thoughts were bouncing along the motorway and invading the smooth leather interior of his car. Her eyes clouded over as she stared at herself. She was afraid of losing Nick. That was what it boiled down to.

'I heard words.'

Tony was already at the table as she walked into the breakfast room and Victoria grimaced at him.

'Just Nick enforcing his will on the weak and innocent.'

'So what does the weak and innocent have to do that she would rather not?' Tony grinned up at her and Victoria pulled another face.

'I have to go to his engagement party. But I'm not through yet,' she added fiercely. 'I may still be able to get out of it.'

'Vick! You can't!' This time Tony looked serious, and she sat opposite, frowning at his change from laughter to shock.

'Why can't I, Tony? It was just an invitation and, like with any other invitation I wanted to turn down, it's simply a matter of a polite refusal.'

'It's family,' Tony reminded her rather sternly. 'It would look very odd if you didn't turn up.'

'I'm not actually family,' Victoria pointed out quietly. 'In the normal course of events I would only have met you all for holidays, and those would have been few and far between. I'm only here because I had nowhere else to go.'

Tony stopped eating and sat back, his face as grave as Nick's. There was a great similarity between the two brothers, but Tony did not have the rather austere, uniquely handsome features that marked Nick out from everyone else. He didn't have the stunning grey eyes, the heavy dark hair. His open and sunny face was now edged with anxiety.

'You've lived here since you were twelve. Don't let Mother and Father hear you talking like this. To them, you're a daughter. It's been a long time. We all thought you were happy.'

'I am!' Victoria protested restlessly. 'I always have been. And don't ask me why I'm behaving like this because I just don't know. It's probably because Nick and I don't get on very well any more, and to have to face this party with those people is just too much. Why should I? I want to slide out of it, let it pass and forget the whole thing.'

'Well, you can't,' Tony stated firmly. 'If you're like this for the engagement party, what are you going to be like for the wedding? You may as well get to know Cheryl's parents now. She's probably going to want you to be a bridesmaid.'

Victoria looked at him in horror.

'I will not! The idea of Lady Ashton fussing and looking me over with displeasure is just too much to contemplate. I can't stand the woman.'

'Nick isn't marrying Cheryl's parents,' Tony insisted. 'Cheryl's nice enough.'

Victoria nodded glumly, unable to dispute the fact. There was nothing really wrong with Cheryl Ashton, except that perhaps she was a little too withdrawn—not surprising with parents like that.

'Well, then, it's just two events,' Tony soothed. 'Soon over, soon forgotten. Sleep on it, with a leaning towards acceptance. Don't do or say anything drastic in the meantime.'

'You sound like a solicitor,' Victoria said disgustedly, and the old smile came back to his face.

'Do I really? I must be improving. It's age creeping on. *You* are a mere babe as yet. You'll learn to be more flexible with the years.'

'I think you mean more obedient,' Victoria pointed out grimly, no more settled about this affair than she had been earlier. If anything, Tony had alarmed her further.

She had never thought of the wedding and her part in it. Seeing Nick get engaged was too much; attending his wedding would be impossible. 'Nick expects you to hold my hand and see me through it,' she finished irritably.

'Providing there are no glamorous ladies to take my eye, I can manage that very well,' Tony promised glibly, and she could see from the expression on his face that he considered the whole matter to be settled. It was easy enough for him. He was a much more placid character. She was more like Nick.

The thought shocked her. More like Nick? She was nothing of the sort! She was quick-tempered but easily hurt. Nick was cool, far-seeing and more clever than she could ever hope to be. She was not at all like Nick; she had just moved in his shadow for twelve years. Now he imagined the position so well established that she would give in about anything.

'How do you think of me, Tony?' she suddenly asked.

'Beautiful, amusing, bright—and sometimes annoying.'

'I don't mean that,' Victoria corrected fretfully. 'I'm talking about on a personal basis.'

'Oh, I see!' He glanced up and then smiled as he saw her rather tight expression. 'I think of you as a cross between a sister and a good friend. You and I haven't changed much, Vick.'

'No, we haven't,' she agreed solemnly. 'Nick was the one to change. He doesn't think of me as a cross between a sister and a friend. I'm just a necessary nuisance from the past. He can't bear to look at me.'

'You're being dramatic,' Tony sighed. 'You were, in any case, never Nick's friend. He was a good deal older than either of us. He's always looked out for you and you know it. It's probably because of Nick that you expect all your own way. There was an element of spoiling in his attitude that did not extend itself to me. I suffered agonies of jealousy.'

'Oh, *honestly*!' Victoria stood and prepared to leave. Tony was grinning all over his face and this was a quite pointless discussion. It was also rather undignified. If anyone else had been listening she knew her face would have been as red as a rose. She knew perfectly well how Tony thought of her. Nick was the problem. It was a good thing their parents had been away for two days. They wouldn't be back until tonight.

Driving down the motorway, her uneasy thoughts still clung fast. Muriel and Frank King were not her parents but she was settled into the family, and it was only when she had a fight with Nick that her real position at Clifford Court came into her mind.

Her own parents had been killed in an accident when she was almost twelve, and that was when she had gone to live at Clifford Court. Muriel King had been her mother's best friend and they had taken her because there was nobody else. Muriel had nursed her through the dreadful shock of losing her parents, but in all fairness she had to admit that Nick had been her real refuge. Older than Tony, he had been a constant anchor, someone to run to, and in those days the dark grey eyes had smiled at her.

It was probably his important position that had changed him. In many ways, he lived in a hard world that she never saw. His reputation was growing and one day he would probably get a knighthood or something. And it wasn't just his attitude to her either. She had to admit that. He seemed barely able to summon up a smile for anyone these days. He had even looked grim when Cheryl had come over to have dinner last week. They would make a rather odd couple.

Victoria tried to imagine them together, having fun. She couldn't quite picture it. Cheryl was tall, slim as a reed, her dark brown hair always in exactly the same smooth style. She didn't have to look up far to meet Nick's eyes. Victoria had to look up a long way because she came just about to his shoulder. Even so she had never felt inferior to him—until now, and that was his doing.

He also managed to make her feel untidy, as he had done this morning. Her own hair was never in the same style. It was fair, curly and behaved exactly as it wished. It was probably too long. Cheryl had short hair.

Victoria muttered irritably to herself. Why this tendency to compare and contrast? She hadn't the slightest wish to look like Cheryl. Besides, there wasn't a lot of spirit there. Cheryl had probably been crushed by a domineering mother. She just drifted along behind Nick and smiled softly. It was a miracle he wasn't bored to tears.

'It takes all sorts,' Victoria muttered to herself as she manoeuvred her way into the car park at work. She would have to put Nick right out of her mind—*and* the wretched party. Today was going to be a busy day. She had to do the presentation for the Winton and Smith account. If they didn't like it, she was in trouble.

'Good morning, Miss Weston.' The secretary greeted her with a smile as she walked in. 'Mr Parker wants to see you. He's in his office.'

Victoria nodded and breezed into the first office on her left. She had no problems with the boss. They were on exactly the same wavelength.

'Ready for the fray?'

Craig Parker looked up with a smile as she walked in and Victoria fixed her mind on work.

'As ready as I'm going to be. We've got to be over in their boardroom for eleven-thirty. Are you coming to watch?'

'I'm not. The nerves wouldn't stand it. This account is worth ten million—if we pull it off.'

'We'll pull it off,' Victoria stated confidently. 'Johnny Gates is just about the best commercial artist in the city. The copy is brisk, amusing and to the point.'

'And you're about the best account manager on the block,' Craig finished wryly. 'All the same, I'll stay here and chew my nails.'

'It wouldn't be the end of the world if we lost this account,' Victoria pointed out severely. 'We've got plenty of others.'

'But this is the biggest so far, and big brother is hyperventilating.'

Victoria grinned. Alfred Parker never set foot in the place but it was his money that had started Craig off. If they got this account he could be paid back and he would be off Craig's neck. She knew what he was like. He had whinged about taking her on when she had left university. Apparently, she was too young, too pretty and looked a bit frivolous to him. It was the curly hair again. Not that it mattered. They were not going to lose the account.

'How do I look?' Victoria gave a twirl in front of Craig's desk and he covered his eyes.

'Mercurial! Too self-confident. Don't antagonise them.'

'I'm talking about the clothes!' Victoria protested.

'Oh! Lovely, smart, expensive. Dark blue suits you, especially with that red, yellow and white scarf.'

'I don't look a bit like an air hostess?' Victoria asked a little anxiously.

'Not like anyone who ever helped me to board.' He was laughing again and Victoria decided to quit while she was ahead. In any case, the suit was new for the occasion and she knew it looked good, smart, businesslike and just slightly glamorous. She should have been wearing this when she tackled Nick this morning. Instead she had been in the usual jeans and sweater. Nick again! She frowned and Craig picked it up at once.

'What's the matter?' He stood up to worry more comfortably and Victoria shook her head at him.

'Nothing about the account,' she assured him. 'It's only a personal problem. Stop worrying. I'll be back before you know it and we can celebrate.'

'If you pull this off, Victoria, I'll give you an extravagant bonus.'

'I should just hope so!'

She made for the door as she saw Johnny with his huge portfolio of artwork, and they turned to the outer door in step.

'The video,' he grunted. 'Stick it in your bag. Lose that and we're finished.'

'We are not finished whatever happens!' Victoria stated firmly. 'You're as bad as the boss. I'm really surprised. You know I could talk my way up a rock-face without a rope.'

'You can talk me into anything,' Johnny agreed uneasily, 'but this will be a full boardroom—men in expensive suits.'

'I've seen expensive suits,' Victoria assured him blithely, holding the door as he struggled out with his burden of huge flip-charts.

It gave her the chance to have another secret frown. Nick had expensive suits. He always looked fantastic. He was tall, athletic, almost aggressively masculine. She'd used to think he was a knight, a hero, a film star. How had he got to be so moody and how was he managing to intrude into all her thoughts? He had to stay right where he belonged—out of her life. Especially this morning. Soon he would be out of her life permanently, and she had better face that fact. A little stiffening of the sinews was called for and right now.

'As you can see,' Victoria said confidently as Johnny finished showing his wonderful artwork, 'we decided to make this completely animated. It's the thing of the moment and has the advantage of being cheaper—no expensive celebrities to hire. The money this releases will be used to spread the campaign further. We already have the preliminary quotes for television and the Press—a wide-ranging cover. The figures are in front of you and I think you'll agree that the costs are very reasonable under the circumstances.'

She paused and looked around as everyone glanced at the sheets in front of them, shuffling the papers and nodding with every sign of satisfaction. They had liked the work too, many of them quietly grinning at Johnny's amusing skill.

'Anticipating your approval,' Victoria went on, 'we have produced a video. This is only the roughed-out plan of action but you will see the characters in the setting and get a good idea of the finished presentation for television. For magazines we will present the last and most dramatic of the paintings. The copy could be changed,' she added, with a glance which said that anyone wishing to improve on perfection would obviously be mad.

Nobody volunteered any ideas and Victoria nodded to Johnny and prepared to enjoy a slight moment of relaxation as the video was shown.

'Phew! You never fail to amaze me,' Johnny murmured as they were once again in the car and heading back to the office. 'I've never seen such a collection of tough old lions.'

'They loved it,' Victoria said confidently. 'During the video-showing there was polite but genuinely pleased laughter.'

'Old Mr Winton was there,' Johnny pointed out in a slightly awe-stricken voice.

'I noted his presence. He tittered.'

'Sure it wasn't disdainful sniggering?'

'The account is ours,' Victoria said firmly. 'You'll see.'

As they walked back into the office Craig Parker met them and gave Victoria a great bear-hug.

'Weston strikes again!' he chortled. 'They just rang— letter of confirmation on the way. We got the account.'

'What did I tell you?' Victoria looked severely at Johnny. 'Have faith, do.'

'I wish I could be like you,' he muttered, his face pink with pleasure.

Victoria gave him a superior smile before disappearing into her own office. She wished she could live up to her working image all the time. The trouble was, it only appeared when she was in action. In any normal setting she felt very vulnerable indeed. She had done so since Nick had withdrawn his affection when she was twenty-one.

It had been a bit like finding that the ground beneath your feet was not too stable after all. Confusion had given way to hurt, and anger had swiftly followed. Now the biggest confrontation of all was on its way, because she had quite decided not to go to this engagement party. She couldn't face it. She could talk her way into or out of anything, so what was so different about this? Deep inside, she knew perfectly well what was different.

There had been a time when she would have simply gone to Nick and begged to be excused from the whole thing. He would have ruffled her hair like he used to do and grinned at her. He would have said, Whatever you want, princess, and that would have been an end to the matter.

He had had that comfortable attitude to her since she had gone to live at Clifford Court, even though at first she had been withdrawn and shocked. Of course she had known them all a little from the past because she had spent several holidays with her parents at the house. Tony, though six years older than her, had always let her tag along with him, but Nick had been different. He was older, more silent, and to her childish eyes terribly important. Besides, he had been at university—a stunning thing to her at the time.

It was only when she'd actually gone to live with them permanently that Victoria had got to know Nick. The tall, dark-haired man with deep grey eyes who had smiled at her and then disappeared had become part of her new life. She was twelve by then, and he hadn't seemed to be so old and distant. He'd still had the same quiet ways that were such a contrast to Tony, but he'd been approachable and she'd soon known that he cared about her.

Looking back, it seemed that she had spent most of the first few weeks sitting in a tree. There was a huge beech tree near the house and she'd gone there every day when she was so miserable and lost. She'd used to climb to the biggest branch and crouch up there, sometimes crying and sometimes just staring out across the fields, too numb with grief even to think.

Nick had cured her of that habit because one day he'd come out of the house and climbed up to sit beside her. Even now she could remember what he'd been wearing: blue jeans and a sweater that was the same colour as his eyes.

'I wonder if this branch is going to crack?' he asked casually when she huddled away from him and said nothing at all. 'You don't weigh much. In fact, you're almost tiny. I weigh a lot more than you, though. Together we must be quite heavy, when you come to think of it.'

Victoria tried to do a rapid calculation of his weight but she hadn't much idea really. What did people weigh when they were twenty-four? He was very tall. She knew that. If you added his weight to hers…!

'It's a long way down there,' Nick mused, leaning forward to look at the grass below, and Victoria's gaze followed his. Until then she had never actually looked down and it *was* a long way.

'You'll have to climb down,' she said urgently, speaking to him for the first time ever.

'I'll go down when you go down,' he agreed, in a comfortable but very determined voice, and she began to feel panicky.

'But I always come here,' she managed desperately. 'I don't have anywhere else to go. I have to think. I have to remember.'

'And do you cry up here, Victoria?' he asked softly, and that was enough to have tears coming into her eyes.

'I—I'm too big to cry,' she whispered. 'I have to look after myself now.' He moved on the branch and she tensed in expectation, knowing it would break off at any moment. 'Oh, please climb down!' she begged.

'I'll climb down if you come with me,' he promised, and she nodded quickly, only too glad to get onto firm ground, her heart beating like a little hammer.

He helped her down the last tricky part but he didn't move away and walk off, instead he took her face in his hands and looked into her eyes.

'Promise me you won't go up there again,' he said seriously. 'You climb very high. You could fall.'

'But I have to think. I have to plan and…'

'You don't have to plan, Victoria. You're twelve years old. You can plan when you grow up. You live here now, with us. And you don't have to look after yourself at all. How about letting me look after you?'

'You wouldn't want to,' she murmured, her shoulders still tense from this unexpected encounter.

'I really would,' he assured her. 'It will give me something to do with my spare time.'

It didn't seem to Victoria that he had a lot of spare time, but she couldn't actually say no so she nodded and went along quietly when he put his arm around her shoulders and led her back to the house. 'If you want to cry, then that's all right too,' he finished softly. 'Just come and find me.'

The tight feeling inside that she had coped with since her parents died began to ooze away, and as she went up to her room she heard Muriel speaking to Nick in a low voice.

'What do you think, Nick?' she was asking, and Victoria stopped on the stairs, a little anxious about his reply.

'She'll be all right,' he assured his mother quietly. 'She's very unhappy but it will pass. Leave her to me. I think she'll come to me now.'

Victoria gave a wry smile. She certainly had gone to him after that, and he had never let her down. She had told him her fears, cried in his arms and listened to every word he'd said. She would have jumped off the end of the world with Nick.

She shrugged angrily. It was a long time ago. She wouldn't jump off the end of the world with him now, but the idea of pushing him off had sneaked into her head from time to time. It wasn't her fault. She hadn't suddenly started ignoring *him* and being icily polite. Sometimes he wasn't exactly polite either. He had grown far away. He was a different person and she wasn't going to start feeling guilty about it. His engagement party had really nothing to do with her, and if he had any sensitivity he would realise that.

CHAPTER TWO

SHE was late getting home. Another client rang just before she was due to leave and Victoria had to stay and take action. Money didn't grow on trees, as Alfred Parker was fond of telling them. Well, he wouldn't be popping in to see about his investment after the Winton and Smith account boosted the firm's reputation with the bank. Craig would be able to pay him off. It was wonderful to be part of a working atmosphere, to know she influenced things. Victoria felt buoyed up, successful.

By the time she walked into Clifford Court it was eight and everyone was having dinner.

'Oh, Victoria, you're back at last! I really was beginning to worry.'

Muriel King's face lost its anxious look at the sight of her and Victoria moved round the table to give her a hug.

'I'm glad you're both back home,' she said. 'The place is empty without you. No more holidays.'

'Never mind us,' Frank laughed, standing to peck at her cheek. 'You look most impressive.'

'Did you get the account, Vick?' Tony asked, and she nodded, giving him a cheerful smile. 'Wow! Ten million! You're big guns now, girl. No wonder you look impressive. If that firm grows it will be all because of you.'

Nick didn't say anything but he was watching her like a hawk. He always was and she tried not to meet his eyes. She couldn't help glancing at him, though, she never could, and he gave her what might have been a smile—although you never could tell with Nick. He might actually be laughing at her.

'Congratulations,' he murmured. His eyes slid slowly over the glamorous suit, lingered on her legs and high-heeled shoes and then scanned over her fair curly hair and Victoria's pleasure faded. He looked sceptical, checking her for faults and no doubt finding plenty. He only had to look at her like that and she felt as if she was playing at life. She had to fight her way out of a sudden feeling of gloom.

'Thank you.' She sat for her meal but she felt awkward now. Her cheeks were flushed and she looked steadfastly at her plate. She had no idea how he'd got her into this state. Half an hour ago she had been important; now she was not much more than a girl.

She was still unsettled later when she went to bed. Nick had disappeared to his study immediately after dinner but his presence had hung around in the air as far as she was concerned. He never seemed to stop working. He never seemed to ring Cheryl either, and she didn't ring him. How odd they were.

He'd used to be the most comforting, normal person in the world, and on the very few occasions she had clashed with him he had always turned out to be right. In those days, of course, he had explained things. He hadn't just gone silent and cold.

She remembered one particular school dance. She had been seventeen, and once every month they were allowed to have a dance in the school hall on a Friday night. It was just a lot of fun but there had been a few romances blooming all the same. She had made the very big mistake of telling Nick about that, and he had just smiled and not taken a great deal of notice.

She had to admit that it had made her feel a bit young and foolish, and when she'd been singled out by one particular boy she had encouraged him, partly out of curiosity and partly out of defiance against Nick.

He'd always come to fetch her after the Friday dance, and this time she had intended to linger, just like some of the others. She'd been outside in the porch and the boy had been kissing her quite vigorously when Nick arrived.

The first thing she'd known of his arrival had been when he touched her arm, making her jump guiltily.

'Time to go,' he advised her cheerfully, although she could tell by the steel in his eyes that he was seething with disapproval.

'I can get a lift home,' she began, but the hand on her bare arm tightened and Nick pulled her towards him with the possessive attitude he usually had.

'You already have a lift,' he pointed out with rather alarming quietness. 'I'm it. Let's go.'

She gave swift consideration to creating a scene, the threat of which usually got her out of trouble, but she had never created a scene with Nick and his eyes told her that he was well aware of her rebellious thoughts and quite prepared to take action. She went, but not very meekly.

'Had a good time?' he asked casually as they drove home. Victoria was sitting grumpily beside him, not caring at all whether her new dress was creased or not. All she could think of was how he had reduced her status, and in front of a boy too!

'I *was* having a good time but you put a stop to that,' she muttered, giving him a nasty look.

'What a shame,' he taunted. 'I didn't realise you were enjoying it so much.'

'It was *wonderful*!' she pronounced extravagantly. 'And it's quite all right,' she added haughtily. 'Christopher is my boyfriend.'

'Well, if I'd known that...'

'You're being superior, patronising, supercilious and condescending!' Victoria raged, turning on him, and he began to laugh, which enraged her even further.

'I doubt if you can even spell those words,' he surmised, grinning across at her.

'I hate you, Nick!' She turned away, moving to the edge of her seat to take her the maximum distance from him, and stared out of the window although she couldn't see a thing.

'Do you really?' To her great astonishment and unease, he stopped the car and flicked on the interior lights. She felt a bit scared at once. She had probably gone too far in speaking to him like that. 'Well?' he persisted. 'Do you hate me?'

'Not often,' she confessed anxiously. 'Only tonight.'

'That's understandable,' he agreed. 'You were having a good time and I spoiled it. Want me to take you back?'

'No! It's too late now.' Victoria gave him a wary look and tried to work out what he was up to. He was pretty important by now, but he still looked after her, and even if he didn't have any spare time he seemed to make some just for her.

'Ah, yes. The moment has passed. I can quite see that,' he mused, and when she looked closely at him she could see his eyes dancing with mischief.

'Don't, Nick,' she begged angrily. 'I hate it when you tease me. You never take me seriously. I'm grown up.'

'Almost. You've still got a way to go, a path strewn with difficulties. When you're grown up—I'll tell you. In the meantime, I'm taking you very seriously.'

'Sometimes,' Victoria fumed, 'I feel as if I'm simply in your clutches.'

'Say the word and I'll drop you,' Nick offered sardonically, but that sounded a bit final and she looked at him from her eye corners.

'I don't want you to drop me,' she muttered. 'I like being special.'

'You are a contrary little pest.' He started the car and she gave him a wary glance but he wasn't annoyed. His lips were quirking as if he could hardly contain his amusement. She gave a great sigh of contentment and straightened her dress, her whole mind given now to the creases that might just spoil it. Nick was back to normal. She could forget everything else.

'Was it really wonderful?' he asked softly.

'The dance? It was quite good. I had my toes stepped on a few times but I bore it with fortitude.'

'I meant the kiss—or kisses. That was the subject under discussion when the word wonderful came up. So was it?'

'Not really.' She shook her head and looked thoughtful. 'It wasn't even interesting actually. It was wet and awkward—all noses. It's not something I'll get into.'

Nick began to laugh outright, and she watched his handsome face and the way his dark grey eyes sparkled.

'What's so funny? Maybe it was me,' she mused. 'Maybe I wasn't doing it properly. Will you show me?'

'Never in a million years,' he grinned. 'Get a book on the subject, or better still, just wait.'

'I'm never going to learn,' she said grumpily, and Nick reached across and took her hand, raising it to his lips and then letting it go.

'Don't rush to grow up, princess,' he advised quietly. 'It will come soon enough but I like you just as you are. As to the kisses, one day it will be perfect with no practice at all. I promise you.'

That was the most comforting thing she had heard all day and by the time they got home, the whole thing had blown over, everything was back to normal. Nick was a knight and she was a princess. Just like always.

What had happened to spoil all that? In all probability she would never find out.

Victoria got ready for her shower and decided to put everything right out of her mind. After all, this had been going on for a long time and she had not made one step forward in discovering why. Perhaps it was because Nick didn't like the grown up person she had become, and there was nothing she could do about that.

The shower was cold, and she sprang out of it as soon as the icy water touched her skin. Now what had happened? This was obviously one of those days. She wrapped herself in her robe and went to investigate, almost bumping into Nick, who looked much less than pleased.

'What the hell happened to the hot water?' he snarled, and Victoria bridled instantly.

'If you think I used it all...!'

'How could you?' he asked scathingly. 'It's supposed to be endless. Nobody suspects you of anything, so keep your shirt on—or whatever it is.'

'It's a robe!' Victoria snapped, bristling with rage and embarrassment.

'Really? I thought robes trailed on the ground and swished silkily.'

'This is short.' Her face was now flushed and she felt idiotic again, furious with him for bringing this on. He could make her feel stupid with just one throw-away remark.

'I noticed. However, when I almost step into a freezing shower my mind pinpoints just the one thing—what happened to the hot water?'

'Well, don't expect an answer from me. I *did* step into a freezing shower.'

Nick muttered in annoyance and moved along the passage towards the cupboard that housed the hot water tank and a variety of switches that Victoria had never quite mastered. She trailed along behind him, only just then noticing that he was not wearing a shirt.

All the same, her eyes moved slowly over the brown expanse of his shoulders. He was more like an athlete than a barrister and she remembered the flashing shots at tennis she had seen him play, well out of her league. She wondered how many ladies went into the witness box and watched him with admiring eyes before his cool, acid tones devastated them.

He opened the cupboard and grunted with annoyance.

'Mother's cleaner up to her usual sabotage, I expect,' he muttered, flicking a switch. 'The pump's off. One of these days she'll blow us all sky-high.'

Victoria stood biting at her lip, her mind swinging wildly between visions of them all flying through the roof and the unusual sight of the rippling muscles on Nick's back.

'You'd better have a look at this,' he insisted rather testily when he turned, and she just stared at him. 'If you're in alone and this happens again you'd better know what to do.'

'Er—I'll find out then,' she got out hastily, bringing her mind swiftly back from the rather glamorous court-room scenes it was inventing to the immediate present. Her wrist was seized in a hard grip as Nick pulled her forward.

'You've never found out in the twelve years you've been here. If you fly heavenward I'd rather it was be-cause of the force of your temper and not because of your inability to flick the correct switch.'

Against her will and better judgement, Victoria found herself being almost propelled into the cupboard.

'That switch there,' he pointed out. He switched it off again. 'No noise now, but when I switch it on again the pump starts.' He gave her a demonstration and Victoria found herself breathing uneasily. It was a long time since she had been so physically close to Nick and it just wasn't right any more. He wasn't her friend, her hero, her mentor. He was different. Besides, he was getting engaged.

'Pay attention,' he ordered when she stood with unnatural stillness, like an uneasy mouse. 'I must have shown you this five or six times during the course of your fluffy-headed teenage years. If you can get a ten million account you can switch a pump on.'

'Look! Just leave me alone!' She snapped out at him and then felt even more flustered when Nick reached for her and pulled her towards him. His arms were altogether too strong and his chest was too close. It managed to scare her badly, especially when she discovered an inclination to stay there. 'And I'm not fluffy-headed,' she finished angrily. 'The only thing that's wrong with me is my inability to put up with your domineering manner.'

He let her go at once, and Victoria dared not look at his eyes. She knew they would be dark and stormy. She had behaved in an idiotic manner, creating a fuss out of nothing, and she was utterly ashamed of herself.

'You won't have to put up with me for much longer, will you?' Nick asked quietly. 'Pretty soon you'll have all the space from me you desire.'

She was sorry then—sorry she had spoken.

'I don't really want...'

'You never seem to know what you want at all, Victoria. When you suddenly find out it will probably be too late.'

She didn't know what he meant, so she stepped clear of him and hurried off to her own room, wishing she had taken an invigorating cold shower and never had this upsetting encounter. Her heart was thumping madly, and in spite of her annoyance she found that tears had come to the corners of her eyes.

If Nick had been an idol who had fallen it would have been a different matter, but nothing like that had happened. He had simply cut her out, leaving her with this vaguely worthless feeling.

He was like a condemning stranger, and although she had searched her mind long ago for any reason there was nothing she could come up with. It was as if she was playing two parts; a vigorous, successful person at work and an anxious and bad-tempered person at home.

And he was not going to be out of her life. Instead he was bringing Cheryl Ashton into it. Maybe she would have to leave here herself, because it was very easy to imagine future meetings, with Cheryl's quiet, un-emotional ways and Nick's indifference. Just thinking about it set her on edge, and she wasn't sure if she could cope without causing upset in the family.

It was probably better to go. She was doing well at work. She could afford it. In any case, there was the money her parents had left in trust for her. She hadn't touched it, but this was beginning to seem more and more like an emergency and she was sure they would have approved of her plans. The trouble was, she had always been happy here—and there was Tony. Leaving Tony would be hard. They were almost like twins, in spite of his extra years.

Over the weekend the hot weather continued, and Victoria did what she loved doing most—she spent her time out of doors. Whether pottering in the garden or walking in the grounds, she was happy out in the fresh air and the quiet at Clifford Court.

At first Frank came with her, and they pulled up weeds and sorted out the plants in the small greenhouse of the lovely old garden at the back of the house. Later, she had a shower and then went out to read in a small clearing under the trees. She wore a bikini and a sun hat and, stretched out on a car rug, she just let the peace of the place sink into her.

Out here it was difficult to dwell on trouble. The book lay beside her unopened, and after a while she closed her eyes and just listened to the sound of the light wind in the trees. She was in the shade at the moment but it was still hot, and a feeling of contentment spread through her and relaxed the tension that had been growing steadily for a good while. She knew she was falling asleep but it didn't really matter.

Her mind turned dreamily to Nick. This court case was one of the most important he had ever faced. There was a dangerous element of the criminal underworld in it. She had sneaked into court twice since the proceedings began, sitting at the back and listening intently but mostly watching Nick. He could turn people round his little finger.

There was a lot of hatred focused on him from the man who was being tried. It showed in his eyes as he watched Nick. She wondered if it was frightening to face all that venomous hate. She consoled herself with the fact that the man was locked up at the moment and tried to ignore the other fact that his friends were not. Still, nobody would dare to threaten Nick King. He was too important.

The sound of voices woke her later, and she realised that she had been asleep for longer than she would have liked. The sun had moved and now it was shining directly on her. When she opened her eyes she saw Nick coming towards the clearing with Cheryl Ashton beside him, and Victoria was too late to beat a hasty retreat. If she jumped up and tried to get away they would see her at once, and she didn't much fancy picking up her things and scuttling off in an undignified manner. She closed her eyes and pretended to be asleep again.

'Oh! It's your sister,' Cheryl said, and Victoria knew they had spotted her.

'Victoria is not my sister,' Nick corrected firmly. 'She just lives here. She's also slightly mad by the look of it. In all probability she's burned already.'

'We'd better wake her up,' Cheryl suggested, much to Victoria's annoyance. They were still not close to her and she considered how to get out of this. Through her thick lashes she could see Cheryl clearly, and the sight made her feel more uncomfortable than ever. Cheryl was, as usual, cool as a cucumber. She wore a very expensive-looking dress and sandals and the dark hair had a glossy shine that spoke of a visit to an exclusive hairdresser.

Victoria felt a little like a child caught playing in the mud.

'Why don't you go back to the house?' Nick suggested. 'Afternoon tea will be ready. I'll wake her and join you in a minute. Getting through to that clearing isn't as easy as it looks. You'll be scratched. Victoria jumps over things or ignores them.'

Victoria felt her blood begin to boil. He just couldn't help it, could he? Even with Cheryl Ashton there he was having a sly dig at her. And it was none of his business if she got burned—none of his business if she was scratched from head to foot.

She kept her eyes closed and prayed fervently that he would go off with Cheryl and leave her to turn a nice, crisp brown. Failing that, she hoped he would tear his expensive trousers as he came through the thick undergrowth. Nobody could infuriate her like Nick. And nobody could upset her like he did either. She could not remember a time when she had been aware of anyone as she was aware of Nick.

There was a long pause, a rather alarming silence, and after a while she just had to take a look. When she opened her eyes, Nick was towering over her. He was watching her silently and she nearly jumped out of her skin.

'The ostrich syndrome,' he murmured scathingly. 'Close your eyes and nobody will see you. It doesn't work.'

'I don't know what you mean,' Victoria assured him haughtily, and he gave her a very ironic smile.

'I'll put it another way, then. You've been awake since you heard us talking. You simply kept your eyes closed. That would be considered childish in some circles but, as it's you, I expected it.'

'I am not childish!' Victoria snapped, sitting up and getting to her feet in one swift movement.

'Embarrassed, then,' he surmised quietly. His eyes ran over her bikini-clad figure and then back to her tousled hair, and his mouth tilted in wry humour. 'It's quite unusual to find something as delightful as this on the edge of a wood. In future, I'll watch out for it.'

Victoria felt as if she was blushing all over, and she bent to snatch up her rug and the discarded book, embarrassingly aware that Nick was still inspecting her with disparaging amusement.

'I can't look cool and sleek like Miss Ashton!' she flared, facing him head-on.

'Did I ask you to?' he murmured softly.

'It's none of your business how I look,' she reminded him forcefully, and he gave one of his elegant, irritating shrugs.

'Then why are we raging? Come back for tea and behave yourself.' He flicked the rug from her grasp and flung it over his shoulder, and before she could stop him he picked her up too and set off for the barrier of branches and tall grass that circled the clearing.

'Put me down!' Victoria stormed, pushing against him.

'I don't want you to be scratched,' he assured her silkily. 'The engagement party is looming up, and you really must arrive at it looking partially civilised.'

'I'll not arrive at it at all,' Victoria fumed. 'I don't take orders.'

'You will on this occasion,' Nick said quietly. 'And as we both know it let's drop the subject.'

She decided to say nothing more, to draw around her what little dignity she had left. She refused to struggle too, although she was excruciatingly aware of how much of her body was visible and how much of it was pressed up against Nick. There was a funny feeling inside her, as if she was choking, and she wondered uneasily if she had had too much sun.

'I can walk,' she managed calmly when they came out onto the lawn at the other side of the trees, and he put her down at once, his gaze running over the slender length of her legs.

'How did you get in there without scratches?' He sounded really intrigued, and Victoria felt extremely smug—especially as he was looking less than band-box fresh himself now, after tackling the undergrowth twice.

'I don't go that way,' she informed him complacently. 'I found another way about ten years ago.' It was her turn to look him over, and she did it with glee. 'Forcing a way through as you did is much too difficult. You'd better slip into something more suitable if you want to match Miss Ashton's sophistication.'

'Her name is Cheryl.' Nick's gaze locked with her dancing blue eyes and Victoria gave him a brilliant, mocking smile.

'Oh, I know, but we don't really know each other. Best to keep it formal. I think she's Miss Ashton and she thinks I'm your sister.'

'You're nothing of the sort!' Nick grated, and she knew she had got under his skin with ease.

'Oh, *I* know it and you know it, but clearly she doesn't,' Victoria reminded him airily, and by now he was not at all amused.

'So you *were* awake,' he concluded with a frown. 'What did you hope to hear?'

'I hoped to hear you both disappearing into the distance, but of course my hopes were dashed because you still insist on interfering in my life. Just stay with Miss Ashton and keep out of my way.'

'I never try to be near you,' Nick pointed out angrily, grasping her arm to stop her walking off.

'Then why are we constantly clashing? Let me go, Nick, and get on with your life. I'm happily getting on with mine and I don't need you to tell me what to do. In fact, I don't need you at all.'

'Don't you?' His grip tightened and Victoria's heart gave an uncomfortable thump.

'No!' She carefully extricated her arm and walked off to the house, trying hard not to think about the fact that he still stood there watching her angrily. It was the end of a pleasant afternoon, because when she had showered and changed into a cotton dress, and came back to take tea in the expected manner, Nick simply glowered at her and Cheryl looked uncomfortably out of place as usual.

Where would she look comfortable? Victoria asked herself. She came to the conclusion that as far as she could see there was no place on earth. Cheryl was a born victim. It should have made Victoria sorry for her but it did not. Cheryl had decided to marry Nick. She could cope with it in that case. Nick would just order her about and Cheryl would be turned into a meek wife, just as she was a meek fiancée. Victoria told herself she couldn't care less.

She was heartily glad when Tony came in and sat beside her, and before very long they were talking almost exclusively to each other. Nick didn't like that either, she noted, but she was too annoyed to make any effort to gush over Cheryl. Muriel was doing that, and as far as she could see Nick was simply bored and angry. Victoria couldn't think why he ever brought Cheryl here to Clifford Court. It was downright peculiar—as if he had won her in a raffle.

On Monday morning the sky was threatening—black clouds massing from the west—and Victoria felt downcast. The two encounters with Nick over the weekend were lurking at the back of her mind and there was not even a sunlit morning to lift her spirits.

'Disgusting weather prospects for mid-June,' Tony declared as she took her place at the table for breakfast. 'If it's like this for the engagement party, Cheryl's mother will throw a fit. Planning to have some big event out of doors in this country is very unwise.'

'It won't bother me,' Victoria muttered, her eyes on her plate. 'I'm not going.'

'Another unwise decision,' Tony warned. 'You're not going to get away with it, Vick, so just toe the line.'

He suddenly went silent, and she knew perfectly well why. She had also heard Nick's footsteps in the hall but she wasn't sure if he had been able to hear Tony's last remark. For some reason he hadn't left early today, and even without looking round she could feel his presence dominating both of them.

'Continue your conversation,' he suggested as he collected his breakfast and sat at the table, 'or was it too private for my ears?'

There was a cold, sarcastic tone to his voice and Victoria found her chest tightening. Nowadays she often found it difficult to breathe when Nick was there. Sometimes she could fight her way out of it with a fit of rage but this morning she felt particularly defenceless.

Whether it was after yesterday's encounter with him or whether it was the depressing sky, she didn't know.

'Much too private,' Tony said smugly. 'You know Vick and I are as thick as thieves. We have a lot of secrets.'

'I'm aware of it.' Nick wasn't amused, and Tony raised one brow at Victoria as she risked a quick glance at him. She knew him too well to mistake his expression. He didn't understand Nick either.

The cold atmosphere made her mind up for her, though. She wasn't going to spend the rest of her time in this house feeling guilty, or being pushed into her place as a person with lingering teenage tendencies. Muriel and Frank came into the room at that moment and she decided to act right then.

She had to wait a while. Frank wanted to know the latest news from Nick's case.

Tony glanced at Nick. 'I popped into court on Friday to watch you at work,' he murmured. 'I heard a few mutterings. There's a lot hanging on this in the criminal world.'

'Maybe we'll rake a few more in,' Nick said with satisfaction. 'If Kenton goes down he'll not go quietly. He's going to take a few with him.'

'I noticed a number of vicious looks aimed at you.'

'From the defence?' Nick smiled sardonically. 'If you're meaning from the friends of the accused, forget it. They normally glower and threaten. If I paid any attention to it I would never prosecute again. When the case is over they'll disappear back into the woodwork.'

'Is this dangerous, Nick?' his father asked, and Nick gave one of his elegant shrugs,

'No more than crossing the road. Forget it.' He aimed a sour look at Tony and then turned the talk to the weather, but Victoria had noted Tony's worried looks. She glanced at Nick but the look she got back was simply bland and indifferent—as usual. It quite made her mind up for her.

She brought up the subject of a move. Craig had been mentioning it for quite a few days, but so far she had done nothing about it. Suddenly she felt that she must go, get away from Nick. She didn't really want to understand how she felt, but she knew it had to stop.

'I've got the chance to move into a really nice flat,' she said quietly, looking at Muriel. 'It's not far from work. I'm giving it serious consideration because the traffic is terrible, and when winter comes things will be worse. It would be the sensible thing to do.'

Obviously it was a bombshell of significant proportions, because all conversation stopped. Everyone stared at her and Victoria knew without looking that Nick's handsome face had gone dark with rage.

'Are you sure, dear?' Victoria's heart sank as she heard the tremble in Muriel's voice and saw the quiet shock on the faces of both Frank and Tony.

'No—no, I'm not sure,' she managed, trying to keep bright. 'It's just that the subject came up and I've thought about it. Er—Craig Parker mentioned it. He's got a flat in the same block and this one is going to be vacant soon. It seemed like a good opportunity.'

'How would you cope in a flat, Victoria?' Frank King asked quietly when Muriel seemed unable to speak. 'You spend all your spare time out of doors. You always have done. You love this house and the grounds.'

'I know,' she assured him miserably. 'I'm twenty-four, though. Maybe it's time that...'

'Leave and I'll dig a hole and jump into it,' Tony said roughly. 'You're the apple of my eye, the cream in my coffee, the milk in my tea.'

'Oh, Tony!' Victoria gave him a grateful smile and managed a wavering laugh. 'It was only an idea.'

'A damned silly one!' he grunted. 'What do you think, Nick?'

'I long since stopped trying to give Victoria advice,' Nick said icily. He put down his napkin and stood, preparing to leave. 'She's neither a child nor a teenager, and quite capable of taking care of herself. She must do as she thinks fit, and no doubt she will.'

He kissed his mother's cheek and nodded to everyone else—except Victoria. He didn't even look at her and everyone sat in silence until the car had left.

'He's angry,' Muriel stated uneasily. 'He seems to lose his temper quickly nowadays...' Her voice trailed off miserably and Victoria bit her lip, knowing that everyone had been badly hit by her announcement. She had been loved here, was still loved. All this had done was let everyone know about Nick's attitude towards her.

'I won't take the flat,' she said quietly. 'I can see it's upsetting you. Anyway, I suppose I would find it difficult to live in a flat. I love it here too much and I couldn't really cope without you. It was just an idea anyway.'

'A stupid idea,' Tony said loftily. 'I notice there was no statement about missing me.'

He gave her a hard, mocking stare and Victoria grinned at him.

'I would have no one to plot with,' she agreed. 'How could I leave you?'

'First sensible thing you've said today,' he grunted. 'Finish your breakfast and get off to work. If Nick's washed his hands of you, I'd better take over.'

That was what it boiled down to, Victoria mused miserably as she drove to work. Nick had washed his hands of her. He had realised that she wasn't really part of the family, and because of his attitude the realisation was slowly dawning on her too. He was important and she was ordinary. He was marrying into a family that had all the things his future would need: position, important friends. Cheryl would look good, draped on his arm at some function, and she could be trusted not to do anything rash or hare-brained.

Sooner or later they would have no contact at all, and when he visited with Cheryl he would look at her as if she were an intruder. There would be no more running to him with problems, but then she hadn't been able to do that for years. It was quite clear that he considered her to be a burden of some sort and he had got rid of her very skilfully. Putting him out of her life was not proving so easy, though.

CHAPTER THREE

AT TWELVE o'clock, Nick walked into her office and stared at her uncompromisingly.

'Get your coat,' he ordered. 'I'm taking you to lunch.'

'I can't!' Victoria felt the welling up of a sort of panic. He had never done this before, even when she had just started work and they'd still been on fairly good terms with each other. 'It's not time yet, and in any case I—I usually eat on the run because we're busy and...'

'Stop babbling and get your coat!' He wasn't giving an inch and Victoria had a very trapped feeling. Standing up to Nick quietly was not at all possible for her. To hold her own with him she had to shout and wave her arms. She couldn't do that here. Too many people were leaning back in their seats and watching openly. Nick was a very commanding presence and the whole staff seemed to have taken on a collective look of deeply intrigued interest. Including the boss.

'I can't leave the office,' she began, but Craig Parker walked in behind Nick and cut the ground from her away with ease.

'Of course you can,' he insisted. 'Your efforts last week should be rewarded. You can have the rest of the day off.'

'I'd rather have the bonus,' Victoria protested quickly, and he nodded with exaggerated importance.

'You'll get that too. Now off you go, my girl. Enjoy yourself.'

'Er—this is....' Victoria began belatedly as Craig eyed Nick with deepening curiosity. Suddenly she didn't know what to call Nick. He wasn't her brother, and he wasn't even her friend now. She was tongue-tied, and very much aware of the sardonic recognition of this on Nick's face.

'Victoria is a member of my family,' he stated, giving Craig a rather icy glance. 'My mother and father look upon her as a daughter.'

'This is Nick King,' Victoria managed breathlessly, and Craig's interest doubled.

'The barrister? Good grief! I was reading about you this morning. This criminal element in your case is looking dangerous. It was on the early news. They were saying that the police are still looking for accomplices and hoping that Kenton will talk. I didn't know Victoria moved in such exalted circles.'

'She doesn't,' Nick said curtly. 'We try to protect her from the seamier side of life on every occasion.'

He wasn't looking at Craig any too kindly and Victoria felt her face flush. Nick was summing him up after her statement this morning about Craig living in the same block of flats she had mentioned. He probably thought...

'I'll get my coat,' she muttered hurriedly, only too glad now to get out of the office. Craig must think Nick was downright nasty and a dreadful snob. It was something she would face later, when she had thought of a good explanation. At the moment she didn't want things to deteriorate further. She had never been so deeply aware of Nick's power.

'Where are we going?' Victoria stopped outside and looked up uneasily at Nick.

'We'll move further afield,' he said grimly, opening the door of his car for her. 'Too many people seem to be interested in your affairs.'

'They're not going to follow me outside to snoop!' Victoria stated indignantly. 'If you didn't look so superior and important they wouldn't have even bothered to look when you came in.' She knew they would have, though, especially the women, and it was nothing to do with his status. Nick was one impressive, masculine being. She wondered if Cheryl was suitably aware of that.

'Get in the car, Victoria,' he grated. 'If you want a scene we'll conduct it in some sort of privacy.'

'I do not want a scene!' Victoria stormed as he got in beside her and slammed the door. There was the satisfying clunk of the door of a very expensive motor car and she felt able to raise her voice a little. It was always safer with Nick for her to be in a rage. 'I never even wanted to come out to lunch,' she continued hotly. 'I didn't even want to see you at all.'

'I can well imagine it,' he muttered coldly. 'However, you *are* seeing me and I have every intention of keeping you with me for a couple of hours.'

'Have you nothing better to do?' Victoria snapped. 'Isn't there some sort of criminal getting off lightly while you're browbeating me?'

'I haven't even begun to browbeat yet,' he warned harshly. 'I'm saving it until we have a place to talk. I have no intention of losing my temper as I drive.' Victoria closed her lips firmly and he cast her a lightning glance that was all contempt. 'Sulk for a while,' he suggested. 'It will keep you occupied.'

She turned her head away and stared out of the window, the protection of annoyance dying. What did he want? She imagined it was all to do with her arrangement this morning, but one never knew with Nick. He had not been there when she had changed her mind and set everyone's fears to rest. Whatever it was, she had rarely seen him more determined, or more coldly angry.

They seemed to be speeding out of London, and before she had worked out where they were going they were parked by the Thames and it was quiet. A few hundred yards away there was a very interesting-looking old inn, but Nick stopped the car well away from it. He switched off the engine and a rather ominous silence hung between them—a silence she was unable to keep up.

'Well?' she asked in a dignified voice. 'Is this to be a picnic or is there no lunch after all?'

'You'll get your lunch when I get my answers,' he assured her, turning in his seat and watching her with dark grey concentration. 'I intend to get my answers, however long it takes.'

'How lucky that I've got the afternoon off,' Victoria said scornfully. 'I don't have to be back until morning. You have all night.'

'You don't have to be back until I say so,' he said coldly.

'What do you want?' Her heart began to beat uneasily at the intensity of his look, and she had the ridiculous urge to open the door and run.

Her feelings must have shown on her face because his expression suddenly relaxed into quizzical amusement, his lips tilting in a wry smile that was all deriding.

'Ah! The panic of the guilty,' he taunted. 'I usually see that look in court, rarely with my guests.'

'How about with your captives?' Victoria ventured. 'An unwilling guest is a captive, I believe?'

He looked at her steadily, frowning.

'If I wanted to capture you, Victoria,' he said softly, 'I'd make a damned better job of it, and you wouldn't have any chance of escape. I want to talk to you without any scenes and without interruption from interested well-wishers.'

'So talk.' She looked down at her hands, twisting them in her lap, hoping the gesture looked irritated and not anxious. All she had to do was come out with the truth and say, If you want to talk about the flat, I'm not taking it. Somehow, though, she didn't want to give in so easily, even if it would instantly get her off the hook.

If her move to a flat was bothering him so much that he was prepared to give up his precious time to come and take her out, then let it go on bothering him for a while longer. The desire to punish him for his treatment of her these past few years was bubbling right at the top of her thoughts. She wanted to punish him for the way she was feeling too, her mind swinging between tears and rage.

Instead of getting down to chastising her immediately, he leaned back in his seat and stared grimly out through the windscreen. His silence was extremely unnerving, and it had the added disadvantage of making her very much aware that they were quite alone.

Nick was always at the back of her mind. He always had been, like a shadow that refused to go away, and now his very aggressive, masculine presence was threatening to choke her again. In the car he seemed to be too close to her, too overwhelming. She could smell his aftershave, and every time he moved she was aware of his silent power.

'Well, go on!' she insisted. 'You brought me here to rage at me. I can't think of any way to stop you.'

'Tell me about this damned flat,' he commanded, turning in his seat to glare at her. 'Where is it? What is it like? And just how much does Parker come into your reckoning?'

He looked just about ready to explode, and Victoria felt a surge of gleeful power of her own. She had managed to get Nick really rattled. This was not his usual cold refusal to notice her over the past few years. This was deep down annoyance. She was glad, because it had brought him back to life when before he had been just a coldly perfect being who had forgotten her.

'It's a modern block about a mile from the office,' she

informed him with a perfectly straight and innocent face. 'It's purpose-built and sufficiently up-market to soothe any of your sensibilities. I don't want you to start worrying that anyone who knows you will discover that I live in a slum area.'

'If you're trying to infuriate me you're making a very good job of it,' he snarled.

She was instantly silent, though somewhat smug, and after staring at her for a moment with vast annoyance he rapped out, 'What about Parker? Where does he fit into this?'

'He's my boss,' Victoria reminded him stiffly. 'If I want to get into a flat there I have to be sponsored. He's willing to do it.'

'And what else is he willing to do?' Nick snapped.

'If you mean what I think you mean, he's married!' Victoria did some glaring of her own and his lips twisted cynically.

'That doesn't necessarily stop a man having a nice, comfortable affair,' he pointed out coolly. 'I meet men like that daily in my job.'

'He's happily married,' Victoria stormed. 'I've met his wife and she's very nice. Even if she wasn't...and even if he wasn't...it's none of your business.'

She turned her face away but he grasped her arm and tightened his grip when she tried to free herself.

'*You* are my business,' he assured her tightly. 'You always have been. If you imagine for one minute I'm allowing you to go off and get yourself into any sort of trouble...'

'I've not been your business for a long time,' Victoria said, suddenly feeling subdued, 'and you know that perfectly well. You were the one who changed, Nick, not me. You can't come storming back into my affairs now as if we were still as close as we used to be.'

She bit down on her lip and stopped. Any more of

this and something would be said that would prove to be too big a barrier to surmount. There was Muriel to consider, and Frank. Even Tony would not be happy if she refused to speak to Nick ever again.

'I still care about what happens to you,' he said with a sort of dark quietness. 'Some things don't change— can't be changed. What does Tony think about this?'

'He threatened to dig a hole and jump into it,' Victoria said shakily, wondering how she was going to tell him that all this was pointless. 'Apparently, I'm the milk in his tea.'

'I heard,' Nick said heavily. 'I knew already, in any case. Have you considered all the people you're going to upset when you simply walk out, Victoria?'

'I'm not walking out,' she managed in little more than a whisper. 'I'm not taking the flat. I told the others this morning after you left.'

Nick went very still, and Victoria almost cringed when he finally spoke. If his voice had been deeply quiet before it was deadly quiet now.

'You allowed all this angry exchange when all the time you had no intention of taking the flat?' he asked harshly. 'You seem to delight in going out of your way to provoke me. Just what did you expect to gain from this? I suppose the whole idea of the flat was part of some irritating plot? In all probability the flat doesn't even exist.'

He looked furious. He sounded disgusted. And Victoria had to face him head-on.

'There is a flat,' she protested. 'Just what sort of an idiot do you think I am? It just shows your opinion of me, doesn't it? I gave the idea up when everyone was so upset, so stunned.'

'So why allow me to bring you here and make a fool of myself?' he snapped.

'I wanted to punish you. I thought it was about time

you had a taste of your own medicine. What you're feeling now is what I've put up with for ages. It's not very nice is it, Nick, when somebody you've always been close to behaves in a strange and hateful manner and you have no idea why?'

He looked at her for a long time and then his tight expression relaxed.

'Do I behave in a hateful manner, Victoria?' he asked softly. 'Maybe I've changed more than I thought. Don't I get a few good points hanging over from the past? I always cared for you a good deal.'

But he didn't care for her now, apparently. He seemed to be quietly regretful all the same, as if he mourned the past almost as much as she did, and Victoria hung her head to hide the expression in her eyes.

'I suppose so,' she whispered. 'Maybe I'm not quite as grown up as I thought.'

'You are,' he assured her quietly. 'I know quite well how grown up you are.' It was the kindest tone he had used to her for ages and Victoria looked up at him, her expression still edged with melancholy. For a second, his eyes flashed over her face and then he made a great effort to be casual. 'Anyway,' he pointed out easily, 'you're a tremendous business lady now. You're getting a bonus to prove it. Come on. I promised to give you lunch.'

He got out of the car and Victoria followed. She wasn't quite sure where this left her, but at least they were still on speaking terms. Maybe things had even slightly improved between them. If she didn't feel the need to fight him so much then perhaps things would look brighter.

She looked up at the sky. The storm had not materialised but it was still hanging about, threatening. It was a bit like her life at the moment, unsettled and worrying.

'You'll have to take me to collect my car,' she said

as they walked along to the inn. 'Otherwise you'll have to take me home and bring me back in tomorrow.'

'Said like the old Victoria,' he remarked teasingly. 'I'll *have* to! Still the little princess, in spite of your grown up status.'

'But what will I do, Nick?' she asked in anxiety, looking up at him.

'"What will I do, Nick?"' he mocked. 'How many times have I heard that?' He gave a sort of rueful laugh before saying, 'I have to call in at my chambers, see a very infuriating man and then I'm free. If you can bear to come with me for those errands, I'll take you home.'

'I'd rather get my car,' Victoria said uneasily, and he nodded as if he had been expecting that.

'In case you're not speaking to me by tomorrow,' he surmised, and she said nothing else. Actually, it was in case he wasn't speaking to *her* by tomorrow. All the same, it was very comforting to be with Nick again, and on reasonably tranquil terms, even if it was a little like being in the centre of a hurricane. It wouldn't last, though, and she had the feeling that Nick knew this as well as she did.

She sighed unevenly and Nick looked down at her. She could feel it but she did not look up and he fastened his hand in her hair, bringing her to a halt, tilting her face.

'Now what?'

'You'll make me look untidy,' she complained, cringing away, but he kept his hold on her hair, smiling sardonically.

'Impossible. A golden bush is a golden bush.'

'I'm not smooth like Cheryl,' she snapped, yanking her head away from his fingers, and he nodded in agreement.

'You're not at all like Cheryl. She behaves very well at all times.'

'If you're trying to make me feel hurt...' Victoria began angrily, but his narrow-eyed look stopped her at once.

'Could I hurt you, Victoria?' he asked softly. 'It's quite an idea. I would have thought that only Tony could hurt you.'

She stared at him in horror, and he suddenly grimaced, taking her arm and leading her to the door of the inn.

'Oh, come along,' he said in exasperation. 'I'm in grave danger of sinking to your level of behaviour. Nobody riles me like you do, Victoria. I have to constantly curb my desire to pick you up and shake you.'

Victoria set her lips grimly. Nick was quite famous for his cool, unemotional approach. Apparently, if he smiled in court, people got worried. She knew she exasperated him with ease, but it didn't seem to give her any advantage.

'I suppose I'm the cross you have to bear,' she said bleakly.

'You probably are,' he agreed, ushering her into the quiet of the inn. 'We all have one, or so they say. I recognised mine a long time ago. It will be there until I die.'

'Don't!' Victoria pleaded, looking up at him urgently, and he glanced down with a good deal of amusement.

'What are you demanding now, that I surrender my cross? Or are you forbidding me to die ever?'

'I don't like you to talk like that,' she said seriously. 'It may be all right to use those flippant expressions in court, but...'

'I'm never flippant in court,' Nick assured her, settling her in her seat and signalling for the menu. 'I therefore reserve the right to be flippant at will at any other time.' He handed her a menu and began to study his. 'Besides,' he added quietly, 'you really wouldn't like it if I became candid and direct.'

'At least I'd know where I stood,' she ventured hopefully, and he looked at her over the menu, the slate-grey eyes dark again.

'Knowledge is not necessarily a good thing,' he assured her softly. 'Sometimes it's better not to know the truth, especially in a no-hope situation.'

It was all he was going to say on the subject. That much was obvious. Victoria gave a sigh and tried to decide what to have for lunch. She wasn't quite sure what they had been talking about, and going over it in her mind didn't help at all. Nick could twist words round until people were dizzy. There was always panic when he was prosecuting, and small wonder.

'I feel worn and shattered,' she grumbled. 'You turn everything inside out.'

He didn't answer, but when she looked up with a certain amount of indignation he was laughing quietly to himself. She watched him warily, making sure he didn't know. He had changed physically too, and she had never really noticed it until now. She had been too hurt and angry to pay much attention but it was quite clear really. His face was leaner, more aloof, more serious, even when he was amused. She wondered what had happened to make him like that. Maybe it was simply his job, the stress of it.

He looked up suddenly and his eyes seemed to leap out at her. It made her cheeks flush guiltily and his grey glance moved over her face.

'Mourning the past?' he asked astutely.

'Sometimes I do and I suppose that's quite childish.' She shrugged uneasily. 'It's nothing I expect you to understand.'

'Why not?' he enquired softly. 'I mourn the past too in my more melancholy moments. Things change, Victoria, and there's very little we can do about it.'

'I would have hoped you'd stay my friend,' she managed quietly. 'I never really thought that the time would come when you and I...'

'We've changed,' he insisted with a quick return to harshness. 'Hanging onto the past is fruitless. In all probability we're wanting to hang onto separate things.'

She already knew that, but his emphatic words drove home the fact that he did not have even any lingering feelings for her. To Nick she was simply a duty. He seemed to have made that clear. And what was Nick to her? She dared not ask that question too deeply.

As it turned out, Victoria found herself trailing along with Nick because he didn't have time to take her for her car before his meeting with this 'infuriating' man he had mentioned. She had to go with him to his very expensive place of work, and that was a revelation. She had never been there before and had never wanted to. It was slightly intimidating.

The building was old, a bit like an exclusive club where members had to be vetted severely, and as he walked in he seemed to have a bevy of awe-stricken underlings following him with notes. He dealt with them all swiftly, and then deposited Victoria in a very luxurious waiting area. She looked startled when he pointed at her. He was looking at his secretary, however, and Victoria took it to mean that she was to be attended to while he was away.

'Tea or coffee?' It was a rather glamorous older woman who hovered over her, and Victoria shook her head.

'Nothing, thank you. I'll just wait.'

'He won't be long,' she was told soothingly. 'Mr King will deal with this quickly. The client is already waiting in his office.'

Poor man, Victoria thought, glad that she was not the one facing the tiger in his own habitat. Being with Nick this afternoon had left her quite shaken. Even when he wasn't speaking there was a power radiating from him that left normal mortals feeling jaded. She leaned back and closed her eyes, willing herself to relax. She wanted no more arguments today. It would be wonderful to go back a few years, to the time when she and Nick...

'Victoria!'

Nick's deep voice penetrated the hazy sleep she had fallen into and she opened her eyes quickly to find him leaning over to wake her. There was a very strange expression on his face and she struggled upright, feeling all manner of guilt at her lapse. Few social graces. That summed her up in a nutshell. She looked round uneasily, greatly relieved to find that no one was about.

'I went to sleep,' she explained self-consciously. Nick had straightened up and now stood looking down at her, his expression back to normal. There was derision in his eyes, and the look that had surprised her before had gone completely.

'Just like Goldilocks,' he murmured. 'We'll get your car now, if you still feel capable of driving.'

'I do. It was only a—a catnap. I'd like to get back before this storm breaks.'

Outside, the sky looked more threatening than it had done earlier, and Nick followed her gaze, frowning at the low black clouds.

'You're unlikely to manage it. It's hung around all day and sooner or later it's going to hit us. However, I'll be behind you all the way.'

'In *that* car? You'll be past me in the first few hundred yards.'

'Not if I choose to trail behind you,' he murmured drily. 'Come along. I wouldn't want to get to your office and find the car park locked.'

Victoria had not thought of that, and minutes later she was hurrying out, trying to keep up with Nick's longer strides. Ridiculous thoughts were chasing through her mind. If it poured with rain before they got to his car, Nick's expensive suit would be soaked. If she had to stop suddenly when he was following her, it would write her car off and dent his car sadly.

'I'll have to be careful,' she muttered to herself, only realising she had said it aloud when Nick looked at her quizzically as he helped her into his car.

'Such a change of character would be too difficult. Don't even bother trying,' he murmured, and her cheeks flushed brightly. He seemed to be driving her mad. Maybe that was his intention. He shouldn't be allowed to prosecute anyone, however bad they were. He was devilishly clever and it wasn't quite fair.

She set her lips grimly and took a deep breath, getting a slanting look from Nick that wasn't entirely amused. He was probably thinking that she was about to start again on the subject of his engagement party. She wanted to, while she was alone with him, but she didn't quite have the nerve. Besides, at the moment he was speaking to her, and that was something not to be cast aside foolishly. Later she would bring the subject up, when the time was a little more appropriate.

'I've been worried about you, Vick,' Tony said as Victoria and Nick walked into the hall at Clifford Court. They had arrived together due entirely to Nick dropping his speed to match hers. As yet the storm had not broken, but it was now so black, so angry as to be almost frightening. It was not even five o'clock and the sky was as dark as night.

'Is that why you dashed home before time?' Victoria laughed. 'I've got a good excuse. I was given the afternoon off. What's your story?'

'A cancelled appointment. I thought I'd get here first and come out for you if things got bad.'

Tony had his usual grin in place and Victoria knew

he was simply teasing. They behaved like this all the time. Unfortunately it did not amuse Nick.

'If you treat her like this she's never going to be able to take care of herself,' he snapped. 'Victoria is no longer twelve years old. She grew up a long time ago!'

He walked off and Victoria looked after him in some astonishment. Hadn't he wasted his day searching her out and demanding explanations about her move to a flat? Hadn't he been furious at the idea that Craig Parker might have designs on her? And what about his slow and boring journey home as he drove behind her like a severe sheepdog?

'What's his problem this time?' Tony asked as Nick took the stairs two at a time and moved out of their sight.

'Who knows?' Victoria muttered, looking a little apprehensive as the lights dimmed and then became bright again. 'If you manage to fathom him out, let me know.'

'Let's have a cosy cup of tea,' Tony suggested, draping his arm around her slender shoulders. 'As a matter of fact, I really was a bit anxious about you. Mum and Dad got back half an hour ago. They're in the sitting room. I know Mum was worried but she didn't say anything. Come and show your beautiful face. She's only going to relax when she knows that all are safely gathered in.'

'Do I really have a beautiful face?' Victoria asked mischievously, fluttering her lashes at him.

'The best in the business. Didn't I say I'd hold your hand at the engagement party?'

The grin left Victoria's face rapidly as she looked up and saw Nick on his way down the stairs. He had already changed into grey trousers and sweater, and the expression on his face told her that the afternoon's truce was quite over. He looked as black as the threatening sky.

He did not come in for afternoon tea either, and later, as Victoria went up to her room to change for dinner, she could hear him talking in his study. It was a phone call, and for once Cheryl was getting the benefit of his attention.

'It's going to be all right,' he was saying. 'I don't want you to worry, Cheryl. It's what we want that matters. Everyone else can go to hell.'

Nick didn't sound particularly soothing, in spite of his words, and Victoria shuddered, feeling surprisingly sorry for Cheryl. If ever she had to run to Nick for comfort he would be so devastatingly logical, so calm and cool. He was always like that now, and apparently he was just the same with his fiancée.

Victoria went slowly up the stairs, frowning to herself. He hadn't always been like that. She could remember dashing to him with all sorts of nonsensical worries. He had sorted them out and soothed away any fears. She sighed. It was power, in all probability. He could not afford to be wrong so he never was, and it had changed him.

What had he said to her when she had called him hateful? 'It's the company I keep.' The Nick she used to know had completely disappeared, and he could never come back either. It was a very mournful idea. It wiped away any annoyance and somehow made the impending storm more menacing.

As they were having dinner the storm broke with a great crack of thunder that seemed to be directly over the house, heralding its arrival.

'Well, it's been announcing its intentions all day,' Frank King said after a glance at the window. 'Now we can settle down to enjoying it.'

His eyes were twinkling as he looked at Victoria and she made a face at him, trying to appear cool when actually she was fairly well scared. It was only just beginning and here she was, as frightened as she had been as a child.

'She's grown out of all that,' Tony insisted in her defence. 'She understands the mechanics of it now.'

'In any case, it's not kind to tease her about it,' Muriel King said with a stern look at her husband. 'You're home now, dear,' she went on, smiling reassuringly at Victoria. 'Safe as houses.'

Victoria smiled back brightly. The trouble was, she had never been quite convinced that houses were safe in times of storm and tempest, so it was a sentiment that did not exactly sit easily in her mind. She had an unnatural fear of storms and it had never gone away

'Had you been in a flat,' Tony reminded her severely, 'I would not have been there to shield you from terror, should terror arise.'

She knew that terror was going to arise the moment she was by herself, and, glancing up, she met Nick's eyes and quickly looked away. He also knew that she had not grown out of her old fear. As to Tony shielding her—he would be fast asleep the moment his head touched the pillow.

It went on all evening, fading in the distance and then coming back right over the house. Finally, it was impossible to linger downstairs any longer without looking extremely foolish, and Victoria said goodnight and went to her room. By now, everyone had forgotten her phobia, but a quick peep through the curtains warned her that all was not over yet and she was by herself. She got into bed with nothing on her mind but the desire to be like Tony and sleep through anything that might decide to come later.

She didn't manage it. It must have been well after midnight when a terrifying crack woke her up. She was astonished that she had slept at all, but there was no chance of ignoring things now. The storm was directly overhead, and when she tried her bedside lamp it refused to come on.

The room was lit up time after time with brilliant light, and the explosive sound she heard next was enough to have her leaping from her bed and making for the door as fast as she could. There was a sulphurous smell and then the sound of falling stones, and Victoria was sure that her worst fears had finally come to pass. Houses were not safe at all.

She ran into the dark passage and dived into the first cupboard she came to. It wasn't difficult to find. This was her old refuge. It might not be a very staunch shelter but it was comforting, a cave for an animal in distress. She had been in here many times in her life at this house. She might not be able to fathom the switches but she knew the security of the warm cupboard, and the feeling of safety she had when the door was closed on her.

She sank to the floor and drew up her knees, folding her arms tightly round them. She could still hear the storm but it seemed to be distant, not so determinedly hunting her as it had been before. Her shoulders relaxed and she gave a shudder. Nobody knew she was here and that was a very good thing indeed, because the image she presented now was definitely secret. There was nothing left of the vigorous Victoria Weston who could talk her way up a rock-face without a rope.

CHAPTER FOUR

IT WAS the light that woke her later, and she opened her eyes as she heard her name being spoken softly.

'Come on out, Victoria.'

She blinked in the light, looking up to find the door open and Nick standing there. He looked very tall and extremely safe and he wasn't laughing at her.

'The lights came back on,' she said shakily. 'It was dark when...' She made no move to get up, and when Nick said nothing more she explained, 'There was a terrible bang and a smell. I heard something falling.'

'The lightning hit one of the chimneys. It was just about the last thing it did.' She stared at him and he held out his hand. 'The storm's all been over for ages,' he assured her. 'There's really no need to hide in here now.'

'So why...? How did you know I was here?'

'Aren't you always here?' Nick asked wryly. 'I had to wait until the others were asleep. If they knew you dived into the cupboard your image would suffer enormously. Tony may be right that you know the mechanics of the thing but he doesn't quite realise the extent of the phobia. I do.'

When she still sat there, blinking in the light, he reached in and lifted her out with no effort at all.

'Go back to bed before you're discovered,' he warned. He was wearing a short dark robe and Victoria wanted some more information.

'You're not dressed,' she pointed out.

'I normally undress to go to bed,' he explained mockingly. She was in her nightie. There had been no time

61

to get into any sort of robe at all. Nick's hands moved soothingly on her bare arms.

'But if everyone has been up… And how do you know about the chimney? And why didn't they think about me…? I mean…'

'We all looked out of the window at the end of the hall,' Nick explained patiently, speaking as if she had little intelligence and needed a lot of help. He turned her back to her room, urging her along, his hand on her shoulder. 'In the flashes we could see the stones from the chimney. As to you, they imagined you'd slept right through it. Tony was very proud of you. But then again, Tony doesn't know about the cupboard, does he?'

She was too tired to be either embarrassed or cross at his taunting and when they reached her door she looked up at him with puzzled eyes.

'I can't think why you didn't tell them,' she murmured. 'I'm not really bothered about people knowing. I'm scared of thunder and lightning; that's how I am. The cupboard is my bolt-hole. You could have told them. I wouldn't have minded.'

'Why should I tell them? Why should I tell anyone?' He tilted her face and for a moment the dark grey of his eyes held hers. 'When I've gone, no doubt they'll find out by sheer chance. No doubt they'll tell me in great amusement when I come for a visit. For now, though, it's my secret too and I'm keeping it.'

He suddenly bent and kissed the side of her mouth, and Victoria was still staring up at him when he gave her a slow smile and went off to his own room.

She went into her room and closed the door, diving for her bed. It was cold, not nearly as warm as the cupboard, but she was too busy trying to puzzle out Nick's actions to feel any chill. He was the very last person to hug secrets to himself, so why would he keep it to himself and why had he kissed her? She fell asleep still turning it around in her head but as usual she could get no further. Nick always said exactly what he intended and nothing more. He probably always had done that but she had never noticed before. She had just taken him for granted.

To her relief, Nick went off for the following weekend. It was assumed that he had gone to spend the two days with Cheryl at her home but nobody actually knew. He was not in the habit of discussing his plans with anyone and nowadays he was too formidable to be approached with casual queries.

After a restful day in the house, Tony suggested that they go up to town to see a show. He was rather pleased with himself when he was able to get two tickets and Victoria knew she would enjoy dressing up and sitting through a good comedy.

'Stunning!' Tony exclaimed when she went down-stairs to join him. 'I couldn't wish for a more glamorous partner.'

She was very pleased that he thought she looked good. She rarely wore black but tonight she had decided to be as sophisticated as possible. It was a sort of defensive reaction to the last few days and the little black dress with its thin shoulder straps looked really good against her lightly tanned skin. She had a wrap that went with it and even Muriel commented when they went into the sitting room to say goodnight

'Oh! You look lovely, Victoria,' she said with an expression of real pleasure on her face. 'Will you be warm enough, dear?'

'And you were threatening to leave?' Tony muttered as they went out to the car. 'You know she would be very upset if you left, Vick.'

She knew. It had all been a foolish defiance. Muriel was not too strong and she needed no upsets in her life.

'You'll have to go to the engagement party too,' Tony finished, and Victoria nodded.

'I know,' she sighed. 'If I don't, Muriel will be devastated. Anyway, she'll need me to back her up with Lady Ashton.'

'There'll be no trouble,' Tony ordered in a superior tone, and Victoria smiled at him sweetly.

'Unless they make any,' she promised. 'I may have to go but I do not necessarily have to be crushed underfoot.'

'Who would dare?' he laughed. 'Besides, if you look like you do tonight, they'll be too stunned to speak.'

That reminded her to buy a new dress for the party and Victoria felt a little more easy on the subject. For one thing, she had faced the inevitable as Nick had known she would. For another, glamour would be her defence. It should be possible to hide very well beneath a veneer of glamour. She had never actually had to try it but it seemed sheer common sense, and she knew she would have to hide her feelings when Nick got engaged.

They were leaving the theatre later when Victoria saw Nick and Cheryl. The sight of them hit her with a peculiar thump. She had fondly imagined they were safely occupied miles away but here they were. Cheryl looked more glamorous than usual and Nick looked devastating. Involuntarily her hand tightened on Tony's arm and he looked down at her quickly.

'What's wrong?' he asked, his hand covering hers.

'Nothing. I—er—slipped.'

'It's those high heels. If you have to pretend to be tall, stand on your tiptoes. Look! There's Nick.'

Victoria had been hoping he wouldn't notice. She had hoped to manage to get past without any encounter whatever, but now a meeting was inevitable because Tony called out and Nick turned his eyes in their direction.

He smiled briefly at Tony and then his gaze slid comprehensively over Victoria. His eyes raked over her quite mercilessly and she was left with the uncomfortable feeling that she looked quite out of place, had chosen something utterly unsuitable for the occasion, and with little thought she clung to Tony for support.

'Enjoying yourselves?' Tony's cheerful smile didn't slip, but it was obvious that he felt Victoria's sudden anxiety because his arm came round her shoulders in a protective gesture that was certainly not lost on Nick.

'Very much so,' Nick said stiffly. 'Now we're about to finish the evening off with supper.'

'Why don't we all go together?' Tony suggested in his usual friendly way.

Victoria was astounded at the wave of dismay that flooded through her when Nick said easily, 'Why not? Let's go somewhere bright. What about Sampson's?'

Victoria saw Cheryl's face light up unexpectedly at the idea and that surprised her. Cheryl looked too nervous to go to such a place.

'Somewhere bright?' Tony repeated drily. 'I think you mean somewhere noisy if you're settling on Sampson's. Never thought you knew such places, Nick. Still, if it's all right by Victoria?'

'And is it all right by Victoria?' Nick asked silkily when she just stood there without answering.

'Perfectly.' She was well aware that she was being stiffly formal but after the way Nick had looked at her she was not exactly easy in her mind.

Nick took over. 'Leave your car here. I'll get us a taxi.' As usual, Tony simply agreed, and Victoria wished he would sometimes lose his temper with Nick. She wished he would refuse to go to supper with them and say something unlikely, like, Victoria and I are going alone.

There wasn't much chance of either, and Tony was always ready for any sort of party. A jolly get-together was the last thing Victoria wanted, especially when they arrived and she found herself sitting next to Nick. She could not quite work out in what mysterious manner this had come to pass. Tony was deeply in conversation with Cheryl—and that was another thing: Cheryl was definitely lively. She was not listening very much to Tony, her eyes were scanning the crowded room as if she was expecting to see someone important. And Nick was ignoring her. Nobody would even begin to imagine that this was his fiancée.

'What would you like to eat?' Nick asked quietly when Victoria sat as stiff as a poker and tried to look around the room with some of the animation that Cheryl was showing.

'I'm not really hungry,' she managed coolly, but he ignored her tone of voice.

'You don't have to be hungry. People come here to dance, make a lot of noise and nibble at things, so what will you nibble?'

'I don't really want...'

'All right. I'll order for you.' His hand flashed up and a waiter appeared like a genie from a bottle. It irritated Victoria. Things always went right for Nick. She glared at the waiter, who blinked at her in surprise and then gave Nick all his attention.

'Nice to see you here, Mr King,' he said, and Victoria sighed aloud. Everybody knew Nick. If they didn't know him personally then they had read about him in the paper. Being with Nick was like stepping into the spotlight. She wondered how many people in this crowded place were surreptitiously watching him.

'You shouldn't be here.' The words burst out before she had time to think, and as Nick turned back to her Victoria's face flushed with embarrassment.

'Why? Have I done anything wrong, annoyed you yet again, started a quarrel?'

He looked quietly amused and Victoria lowered her voice, well aware that the waiter was now with Tony and Cheryl.

'I was thinking of this court case. Anybody might be here. How do you know that that man, Kenton, hasn't got people watching you? They might...'

'Calm down, Victoria.' Nick's hand covered hers on the table. 'It's not the first time that I've faced hostility in court.'

'This is more than that, though. These people are criminals. That man must have somebody watching you, waiting for a chance to... If anything happened to you...'

'Somebody else would pick up the banner.' His hand closed round hers warmly. 'The people I prosecute are *always* criminals, Victoria. This case is no different. It's just bigger than usual and has attracted more news coverage. There are always friends and accomplices lurking in the background, however. Not really any different from now.'

'I never knew.' Victoria whispered the words, and Nick suddenly used the hand he was holding to pull her to her feet.'

'We'll dance until they get around to serving us,' he said firmly.

'What about Cheryl?'

'Cheryl will be disappearing for a while. Don't worry about her.'

They were out on the crowded floor by now and Victoria looked up at him in astonishment.

'She'll be disappearing? She's your fiancée! Don't you care?'

'Only vaguely,' Nick murmured, swinging her into his arms. 'I know where she's going.'

'Where?' Victoria demanded, but he simply pulled her

close and started to dance. She had to follow whether she wanted to or not.

'She's meeting somebody,' Nick told her, in such a casual voice that she pulled partly away to stare at him again. He just looked back blandly and Victoria felt her annoyance rising.

'You two are the most peculiar, the most odd, the weirdest couple I have ever known!'

'Some people would take that as a compliment,' Nick told her, bringing her close again.

'Not unless they were as odd as you!'

'Hush, my princess. I'm not about to waste precious time arguing.' His hand slid to her back and he held her tightly against him. She could feel the warmth seeping into her and her own rising desire simply to accept it almost overwhelmed her.

'This is not r-right,' she managed shakily, and Nick growled like a disgruntled tiger, his voice almost in her ear.

'Why? You said yourself that we used to be close to each other. Do you really think I want you out of my life? I'll never let you go, Victoria.'

'Please, Nick!'

Her head was swimming and faintness threatened to get the better of her. She knew she was clinging to Nick to stop her trembling legs from letting her down and he suddenly took pity on her.

'Let's see if your nibbles have arrived,' he suggested calmly, and led her back to their table.

He gave her plenty of time to settle down, poured her wine and said nothing at all. Tony was dancing with somebody that Victoria had never seen before, his attention totally on the redhead in his arms, and at any other time Victoria would have laughed. Tony was an apprentice rake, or so he had told her. Right now, though, she wanted him here to give her some safe ground to move on. Cheryl had disappeared and Nick was not at all put out by it.

When two waiters arrived with all the necessary equipment for crêpes and the flames were blazing over the pan, Victoria found the courage to glance at Nick.

'I remember everything you like, everything you have ever liked,' he said in answer to her unspoken question. 'Anyway,' he added in amusement when she just went on looking at him in a wild and puzzled manner, 'it's impossible to quarrel when you're eating this sort of thing.'

Victoria sat and stared at the little flames and watched the waiters. The world seemed to have dropped out from under her. She knew now why she didn't want to watch Nick getting engaged. When he got engaged she would have lost him and the thought was unbearable.

'Drink your wine and stop trembling,' he advised softly. 'You're a big girl now.'

She didn't answer. Tonight she had certainly been shocked into taking that last step in facing herself. If that meant being a big girl, Victoria was not at all sure that she liked it. It hurt too much.

Nick did not leave with Victoria and Tony. He was waiting for Cheryl who had not reappeared when they left. Victoria was still shaken by her time with Nick, and puzzled by Cheryl's conduct. She was silent for most of the journey home, listening only vaguely to Tony's enthusiasm about the redhead and when he suggested a bottle of champagne as a nightcap she was really too numb to protest.

Nick came home after midnight, and by then the champagne was almost finished and they were sitting on the floor, their backs resting against the settee as Tony told another of his funny stories. Victoria was thinking quite muzzily that she was finding it more amusing than the tale merited, at least she couldn't seem to stop giggling, and that was the moment when Nick chose to walk into the room.

Neither of them had heard his car arrive, which was not really surprising, considering their slightly hazy condition, and he stood inside the door and summed up the situation very swiftly.

'Is this your idea of a good end to an evening out?' he grated, his eyes on Tony's grinning face.

'Did you know that you've become extremely stuffy of late?' Tony enquired in a voice that was definitely slurred. To Victoria, he looked unexpectedly cross. Tony was never cross and, given that Nick was looking like her nemesis, she felt very uneasy. It wiped the giggle out of her altogether.

'I'm going to bed,' she announced, struggling to get to her feet. The skirt of her black dress had ridden up well above her knees and Nick glared at her.

'If you're capable!' he snapped.

'Together we are capable of anything,' Tony announced expansively. 'We'll tackle the stairs as one.'

'And roll down to the bottom,' Nick interrupted angrily. He strode into the room and yanked Victoria to her feet.

'If you imagine we're drunk...' she began haughtily, and Nick stared down at her with fury on his face.

'I don't need imagination,' he snarled. 'The evidence of my eyes is quite sufficient.'

'Leave her alone,' Tony ordered, lumbering to his feet and swaying wildly. 'Vick and I will not be separated.'

'Go to bed,' Nick snapped, looking at him in disgust. 'Protest tomorrow, when your head sits more firmly on your shoulders.'

'It's the neck that sits on the shoulders. A person of your status should know that,' Tony began, and then he sat down abruptly on the settee, looking quite vague again.

Nick didn't listen to anything else. He began to march Victoria from the room, and when her legs showed a tendency to buckle he swung her up into his arms and proceeded with bristling silence to take her up the stairs.

'What about Tony?' she enquired uneasily. She was feeling very dizzy, and Tony had drunk a lot more champagne than she had. Neither of them were really used to it and looking back she could see that they had treated the drink very much like orange squash. She had drunk more wine than usual at supper too. It had seemed to be a good way to hide from her sudden awareness, a good way to hide from Nick. She couldn't hide from him now, though.

'I'll deal with Tony when I've dealt with you,' Nick growled. 'If I hadn't come home you would no doubt have still been there in the morning, very much the worse for wear.'

'Well, pretty soon you won't be coming home,' Victoria pointed out solemnly. She draped one slender arm around his neck to help her to balance, very much hurt when Nick seemed to stiffen at this small act. 'When you're married, Tony and I will be quite capable of coping without you. We were coping very well just then.'

'Cope now!' Nick stopped and stood her down swiftly on the stairs, watching her angrily as she swayed and made a grab for him, not trying to hide her panic. At that moment the stairs seem to stretch on for ever, each step a danger.

'Nick!'

'So you need me after all?' he asked harshly, catching her in his arms. 'You always have done so let's stop pretending, shall we?' He swung her up again, and this time Victoria wound her arms around his neck and held on tightly, with no intention of letting him put her down until the floor beneath her had stopped its tendency to dance about.

At her bedroom door she felt a little more secure, and when Nick deposited her on her feet she looked up at him earnestly.

'Thank you,' she murmured in a small, dignified voice. 'Without your help it would not have been possible.'

He stared at her hard and then, unexpectedly, his face creased into smiles, the dark grey eyes sparkled and his voice was filled with laughter.

'Do you think you can actually make it to bed without any further calamity?'

'You used to always look like that—how you're looking now,' Victoria said in a puzzled way. 'I'd forgotten. It's been so long... I wonder what happened?'

'I expect we grew up,' Nick said softly. He tilted her face to the light. 'Can you make it to bed?'

Victoria nodded and started to turn to her door.

'I can manage perfectly well,' she assured him. 'I'll see you tomorrow.'

'I doubt it. I'll be at Cheryl's all day, helping to plan the party. We get engaged at the end of next week, if you recall.'

'I'll hate it,' Victoria announced, looking back at him.

'But you'll go, all the same.' There was no threat, just the complete certainty of her compliance, and Victoria nodded, her blue eyes solemn on his rather saturnine face. Now he was serious again and back to being somebody she didn't quite know.

'I'll go. I suppose we all have a duty after all—a cross to bear.'

'But only on this one occasion,' he pointed out. 'Why do you hate the idea so much?'

'I don't know. It just keeps screaming in the back of

my mind. Maybe it's the fuss of the wedding I'm really thinking about. There'll be all that to go through.'

'Can you face it?' Nick asked softly. He stroked her hair back quite gently but she didn't want that. She didn't really know what she wanted. There was only this terrible depression, as if the world was ending.

'Do I have a choice? I feel trapped by it all—goodness knows why. After all, it's your damned wedding!'

'Yes, it's my damned wedding,' he agreed quietly. His dark head bent and she knew he was going to kiss her again, just as he had done the night of the storm. She also knew it was very wrong, but she didn't try to avoid it. The other kiss had been stingingly sweet and this was the same. It held her in a sort of timeless suspense, although his lips were only lightly touching hers.

'What about Cheryl?' she whispered when he lifted his head and looked down at her seriously.

'Oh, she came back after a while. I knew she would. I took her home.' He seemed to be laughing at her again, and Victoria's forehead creased in a slight frown.

'I didn't mean that.'

'So what did you mean, then?' There was a taunting quality to his voice and Victoria didn't have the courage to point out that she had been asking why he had kissed her like that when there was Cheryl.

'Nothing,' she said lamely, and before he could speak again she escaped into her room.

The effects of the champagne and the wine seemed to have disappeared. She felt uneasy, uncomfortable and unsure with Nick. He had grown light years away from her over the past few years and suddenly he was back, but in such a changed manner. She wanted to cling to him and was afraid to ask herself why.

She sighed and got into bed. One more week and it would be practically over. Nick would have moved to another plane, taken on an added status that was nothing to do with her. He would be engaged.

'What's this about your brother getting engaged?' Craig Parker asked as Victoria went in to work on Monday.

'He's not my brother—and how do you know about his engagement?' She gave him a nasty look. This engagement was becoming a very sore point with her. She hated it, she hated the idea of going to it, and even here at work it was being pushed down her throat.

'Morning paper,' Craig informed her smugly. 'There are no secrets from the Press, especially when a big name is concerned.' He put the paper into her hand, the page folded back for her to see, and sure enough there it was. TOP BARRISTER TO MARRY.

Victoria didn't read any more. Now it was following her to work, just as Nick had followed her to work last week, just as Nick seemed to be with her all the time now. It would be a good thing when all this was over. She turned away, muttering to herself, and Craig watched her in amusement.

'I can see this thing is getting to you,' he observed. 'In a way I can understand. Break up of the family. It always happens.'

'I am not family!' Victoria snapped, glaring at him and walking into her own office, slamming the door behind her. It was a few seconds before she realised just how she was behaving and then she went rather sheepishly back.

'I'm sorry, Craig,' she offered. 'I really don't know what's wrong with me. I'm ready to fight everyone.'

'Forget it,' he soothed. 'Anything like this brings stress into a family.'

'Well, it shouldn't,' Victoria pointed out fretfully. 'An occasion like this should be a joy.'

'Obviously something went wrong, then,' he murmured, giving her a sideways look. 'Maybe you're jealous.'

'What?' She stared at him and he shrugged amiably.

'Think about it. You've had his attention for years, even if he isn't really your brother. Now things are changing. In a way, you're losing him—losing a caring adult.'

'You're not really an analyst are you?' Victoria pointed out in a sweetly sarcastic voice. 'You should stick to what you do best.'

'Well, I worry, but there's not really a career in it.'

He laughed and Victoria shook her head at him in mocking amusement, but she was glad to get to her office all the same. Was she jealous? It was true she had been hurt and angered by the way Nick had behaved these past few years but she wasn't a child. What did it matter? Life would go on, and as to this party she would go to it and hide behind glamour.

It took her the rest of the week to find the dress she wanted. Cheryl and her mother wore expensive designer clothes, but Victoria liked things that were more simple, and in the end she found the dress in a little out-of-the-way boutique.

She knew as soon as she saw it that this was the perfect thing to wear. It was a dark, royal blue made completely with lace that sat smoothly over a satin sheath. The scooped out neckline and tiny sleeves suited her and the skirt was slightly flared. It was quite short but not extravagantly so and she came out of the shop, hugging the box happily. With her fair hair it would look very good.

Nick had been away all week. The big trial was taking all his attention and Clifford Court had been quite peaceful without him. On Friday night he arrived home soon after Victoria, and the engagement party on the following day was all Muriel could talk about at dinner. The weather was beautiful at the moment and if it stayed like that the whole thing would go off swimmingly.

Victoria watched her as she made this statement with satisfaction, and as she caught her eye Muriel smiled happily.

'One day we'll be planning the same thing for you, Victoria,' she pointed out.

'Oh, no!' Victoria muttered. 'I'll sneak off and come back married.'

'Don't you dare,' Frank warned. 'We'll want to put on a show. You're the only one we can do it for. The bride's family get all the glory and we'll just have Tony left.'

'I'll sneak off and get married too,' Tony announced, raising his glass to Victoria. 'In fact, we'll do it together.'

'You're on!' Victoria agreed. 'Let me know when the time is ripe.'

It was their usual bantering, and taken as such by the whole family. Nick didn't look particularly amused, however, and later he cornered Victoria when she was alone in the sitting room.

'No sliding out of things,' he warned darkly.

'I've got the dress and the attitude. Don't worry. I'll be there. I suppose you've come home today to make quite sure that I toe the line.'

'I came home to search for a little sanity,' Nick said moodily. He flung himself down on the settee and Victoria realised that he looked tired. She had never seen him look like that before.

'It's the embezzlement case,' she surmised. 'I was reading about it this morning at work. Even if I hadn't been I would still have known. The whole office is agog with it. Do you think he'll get off?'

'No chance,' Nick muttered blackly. 'How he expected to get away with it is a mystery to me, but he'll not get off if I have to live in court until it's over.'

'He sounds pretty slippery but you don't seem to be having a lot of trouble with him,' Victoria murmured. 'How awful to think of going to prison for a long time, though. Doesn't it bother you? Being prosecuting counsel and striving to get somebody locked up for years must be terrible.'

'Knowing about somebody being tricked out of everything they've worked for is the terrible part,' Nick assured her grimly. 'I look at this smooth customer and I see the faces of all the people he swindled. They're in court every day, looking devastated.' He glanced up at her quizzically. 'Or maybe you think I work like a cold-blooded machine?'

'I spent a lot of time today reading about how clever you are,' Victoria pointed out. 'I suppose I should have been doing a lot of other things but I wasn't. And I wasn't criticising just then either. Don't pick a fight, Nick. Not tonight. It's the last night before your engagement.'

'What's so important about that?' He gave her a sceptical look. 'I'm not taking off to distant parts. I'm only getting engaged.'

'Only?' Victoria stared at him, her blue eyes wide and shocked. 'It's the most important thing, and next you'll be married.'

'Not for ages,' he said shortly.

'Why?' She went on staring at him and he suddenly stood, coming to tower over her.

'What do you care? Or do you want me married and in my own house as speedily as possible?'

'No.' She turned away but he leaned over her to turn her face back, tilting it to the light and forcing her to continue. 'As a matter of fact, I'm finding it all a bit traumatic. Craig says…'

'Go on,' Nick murmured. 'What does Craig say?'

'He says I'm probably jealous because I'm—I'm losing someone from my life,' she blurted out, angry with herself the moment the words had left her lips. They had sounded all wrong. 'He says it's like losing a caring adult,' she rambled on wildly. 'Like when I lost my parents—although it's not really the same, is it?'

'Not at all,' Nick snapped. 'Perhaps Craig should leave that sort of thing to somebody who understands.'

'That's what I told him,' Victoria managed. She had more or less talked herself into a hole but Nick seemed to be ignoring it.

He stood upright, letting her go. 'I imagine you'll be arriving at the party with Tony?'

'I expect so. He's not taking anyone else.'

'He never does. I think we can safely say that you really are the apple of his eye. I'll see you there, then.'

He went and Victoria chewed at her lip. Why was it that she couldn't just chat to Nick? She gossiped to Tony for hours. For a few moments there she had thought things were back to normal, but clearly they were not. The thought of his engagement was not lifting Nick's spirits. His mind was still in court. And why had she told him about Craig's remarks? She really would have to watch her step. Certainly Lady Ashton would be eyeing her closely at the party. She had only seen the woman once, and dislike had been instantaneous on both sides.

Thank goodness for Tony. At least they could whisper together if things got too much to handle. She made a wry face. Too much to handle. Didn't she pride herself on being able to handle people? How was it that she could face a boardroom of sceptical clients and win them over and yet she was dreading one simple engagement party?

She suddenly stood, angry with herself and even more

angry with Nick. She was a person in her own right, important in her own way. Nick could glare as much as he liked. She would go there and simply glitter. She went upstairs to try on her dress and rehearse her make-up.

She was in her dressing gown and just settling at the mirror to test out her skills when there was a knock at the door. She thought it was Muriel, come to do a little fussing, and called out, 'Come in!'

When Nick walked in she just sat looking at him through the mirror, with so much astonishment on her face that his lips twisted in a wry smile.

'It's out of character, I know,' he murmured. 'Your startled face doesn't really surprise me. Did you think it was Tony?'

'I thought it was Muriel,' she corrected. 'Had I thought it was Tony, I would have probably informed him that I was asleep. I don't feel much like a good laugh. I don't feel like a good lecture either,' she added, turning round to look at him crossly.

'I came to apologise.' Nick closed the door and leaned back against it. 'I have no right to take my misery out on you.'

'Are you miserable, Nick? But why? Tomorrow is your big day.'

'Is it?' He turned back to the door but Victoria stood quickly and walked towards him before he could leave. She had the troubled feeling that for once in his life Nick had been appealing to her for help, and she couldn't think what to do.

'It should be,' she insisted quietly. 'It means you're giving your life to the woman you love. Getting engaged is a sort of—of gesture of fidelity, a promise.'

Nick turned to face her, slanting a look of almost scathing amusement at her.

'Maybe I'm not making any such promise.'

'Then you shouldn't be getting engaged.' Victoria's

face flushed with shock and her eyes looked more blue than ever. Nick being fickle, unfaithful, a philanderer? It refused to sink in. 'You don't even mean it,' she accused him. 'This is just another ploy to put me off my stride tomorrow!'

'How could I?' he asked softly. 'I understand from Mother that you've got a new dress and an urge to be glamorous. Add that to your normal image and who could put you off your stride?'

'You could.' Victoria turned away, feeling strangely beaten, going very still when he reached out and touched her arm, running his hand over the silky material of her dressing gown.

'I won't,' he promised quietly. 'I really did come to apologise. I seem to leave you looking either unhappy or angry lately.'

'It doesn't matter,' she said in a whisper. 'I intend to survive.'

'Oh, we'll both survive,' Nick assured her softly, 'so let's say goodnight.'

Victoria turned to look at him and his gaze ran slowly over her face. His fingers lightly touched her skin and then he swept her closely into his arms, kissing her startled lips with sudden urgency.

She didn't try to stop him. These small, unexpected kisses were beginning to disorientate her. When he had first kissed her she had been too astonished to really think, but now she knew she waited for them, trying not to dwell on it too deeply but almost hungry for more.

'Why?' she whispered, too shaken to pull herself out of his arms.

'You know why, Victoria. You're just too scared to think about it.'

'Cheryl...'

'Cheryl is a mystery to you. It will unravel—in time.' He stared into her eyes for a minute and then shrugged and let her go, opening the door to leave. 'Get your beauty sleep because there are going to be plenty of female eyes on Tony at the party. He's not exactly ugly.'

He was gone before she could think of any retort, and after that Victoria had lost all her desire to practise with her make-up. Any encounter with Nick seemed to take the life out of her in one way and excite her to madness in another. The word 'jealous' should never have been spoken. It was running round in her mind and she couldn't dismiss it because it was true.

CHAPTER FIVE

AS USUAL Victoria went with Tony to the party. They automatically did things together. Everybody seemed to expect it and, in any case, she knew Tony well. If she had insisted on going in her own car he would have sulked. He was quite capable of that.

Cheryl Ashton's home was more or less exactly how she had expected it to be. There had always been something comfortable about Clifford Court, something easygoing, like a farm in the country, like a memory of childhood holidays. At Clifford Court there were trees close to the house, flowering bushes, a stream where bulrushes grew unhindered. It was a very natural place that sat easily in its surroundings.

The house where Cheryl Ashton lived was groomed into rigidity, and at the first sight of it Victoria felt her heart sink one more notch. The lawns seemed to stretch to the gates, everything trimmed back and immaculate. They must have an army of gardeners, and everything in bloom was magnificent enough to look unreal.

The beautiful weather had held, and today had turned out to be a perfect day, hot and still, with a brilliant sky that was almost untouched by clouds. It was the sort of day that Lady Ashton would have expected and here it was to order. The marquee was visible as soon as they turned the corner in the long drive and sure enough there was tulle—pink and white. At the moment it wasn't even blowing in a slight breeze—no doubt that had been ordered for later.

'How soon do you reckon we could make moves to leave?' she asked through gritted teeth.

'Let's arrive first, shall we?' Tony murmured, glancing at her uneasily.

Muriel and Frank had set off earlier with Nick, and now Victoria was beginning to wish she had asked to travel with them and been able to arrive in a group. That way she would have been unnoticed. Today she seemed to be filled with the fluttery feeling of unsteady nerves and, in spite of Tony's wolf whistle when she had appeared dressed and ready, she found herself worrying about her dress, her shoes, her make-up and just about everything else.

Weeks ago, she had assumed that her nerves at home were because of Nick's attitude, that her vigorous working manner and her anxious ways at home could be put down to him entirely. Yet here she was now, bringing her nerves with her, and yet she knew she would definitely be in the background today, Nick would be much too busy even to look at her. It was not nerves. It was agony, loss, jealousy.

'I wish I'd stuck to my guns,' she muttered. 'If it were possible I'd just turn right round and go.'

'For goodness' sake, Vick, we're merely guests! According to Mother there are going to be swarms of people here. We won't be playing any significant role until the wedding.'

'And I'm not going to that!' Victoria exclaimed adamantly. 'This has taught me a lesson about instinct. Every instinct told me to slide out of this, yet here I am. I'll miss the wedding if I have to get a job overseas and travel to Nepal.'

'I've never seen you so het up,' Tony told her quietly. 'I'm not doing a very good job of calming you down either.' He stopped the car by the huge, double front doors and looked across at her. 'Nick ordered me to keep an eye on you.'

'What does he think I'm going to do, overturn a few tables?'

'It wasn't like that,' Tony explained patiently. 'It was said in a kindly manner. He just said, "Take care of Victoria." I was going to anyway, as I told him.'

'I do not need taking care of!' Victoria fumed. 'Do you realise that I do an important job and get well paid for it? Do you realise that other people depend on me? If I didn't show up at the office things would grind to a halt. The boss depends on me too, and he's a man! But when I get home I'm nothing—someone to be ordered about.'

'Do I order you about, Vick?' Tony enquired, looking at her through narrowed eyes and ignoring her anger.

'No. It's—it's Nick. I can't stand the way he carries on. I can't stand…'

'You don't need to convince me,' Tony murmured wryly. 'You said the two key words. "It's Nick." I'm not really surprised. It's been coming on for years.' He shrugged his shoulders and prepared to get out of the car. 'There's nothing I can do about it, Vick. Where Nick is concerned I'm powerless. The two of you…'

'Can you park in the courtyard around the back, please?' Before Tony could step out, a self-important-looking man appeared at the open window and spoke severely.

'Tradesmen's entrance? Certainly,' Tony said caustically, starting up and moving off.

'Who was that?' Victoria wanted to know, surprised at Tony's tone of voice.

'A minion,' Tony muttered crossly. 'There'll be hordes of them here. Stop moping about Nick and get that superior look on your face you sometimes wear. It makes me feel important.'

Victoria told herself she was not moping about Nick, although she felt sick inside, and she felt anything but important when they drove round the back. There was a small courtyard at Clifford Court. It always seemed to be full of leaves. This one was full of expensive cars, all parked with mathematical precision, and Victoria's face set stubbornly. She hated the whole thing already and she was still sitting in the car. What would it be like later? The feeling of nausea grew. Nick was getting engaged and she would be forced to watch. Suddenly it seemed like the end of the world.

An hour later she felt jaded and the engagement hadn't even taken place yet. It was hot in the marquee and she had been trying to avoid everyone. Tony stuck by her with grim insistence, but even his cheery smile was a bit fixed, and the few times that Victoria had encountered Nick she had promptly turned away and made for Tony again.

She knew she was behaving in a completely unnatural manner but there seemed to be nothing she could do about it, and the sight of Nick in a grey suit and dark tie made her breathless and uneasy. She seemed to be looking at him all the time and wishing she wasn't.

Muriel and Frank were with Sir Alwin and Lady Ashton, and Cheryl was not looking at all flushed with happiness. In fact, there was more formality and gloss than happiness to absolutely everything.

'This is what I would call a "rum do",' Tony breathed against her ear, and Victoria could only agree. It was all wrong and she didn't know why. It was like a diplomatic agreement. She felt cold in spite of the warm day.

When the engagement was announced by Cheryl's father there was silence at last, and for the first time Cheryl looked a little less taut. She stood close to Nick and he had his arm around her. It was the first time that she had seen them show any sign of affection and the effect it had on her own misery stunned her.

This was it! Victoria realised that she had not really expected it to happen. It had all seemed like a dream before but now it was real, and her eyes fastened on the ring with morbid fascination. It looked hard, cold, glittering in the afternoon sunlight, and she couldn't seem to take her eyes from it.

Something odd was happening to her and she didn't know if she felt sick or dizzy. At first she had wanted him to be engaged, out of her hair, but now it seemed to be such an irrevocable step. The next step would be marriage—the final step.

'I feel faint,' she muttered, and moved towards one of the openings and the fresh air.

'Vick!' Tony moved to go with her but she signalled him back fiercely.

'Stay here. I'm all right,' she insisted. 'I don't want any fuss.'

Outside she simply ran. There was nobody to see her and she fled to the trees close to the edge of the lawn, wishing that this place had some of the wildness of Clifford Court, somewhere she could hide. Her heart was pounding and she put her hands against her flushed cheeks, wondering what had happened to her.

She told herself that it was the champagne, the heat inside the marquee, but that didn't explain the funny lost sensation inside, the awful sinking feeling, the growing dread. She stood with her back to the house and tried to calm down but she felt bereft, as if her life were ending.

'Victoria?'

She gave a guilty start at the sound of Nick's deep voice but she seemed to be incapable of turning with any sort of smile on her face, and when she went on ignoring him, his hands came to her shoulders, warm and firm against her bare skin.

'What is it?' he asked gently.

'I felt a bit faint.' She managed a normal voice and

took a deep breath, preparing to turn and face him. 'There was absolutely no need to come and find me. I told Tony to stay there. I hate fuss.'

'I'm not actually fussing.' He turned her, keeping his hands on her arms. 'You expect me to simply get on with things, knowing you may well be lying in the trees, out to the world?'

'I didn't think anyone would notice. Anyway, I'll be all right now and it's your engagement. You should be there. Cheryl will be looking for you.'

Victoria lifted her head and managed to look squarely at him but he said nothing. His eyes were narrowed and glittering, searching her mind, and she moved uneasily, not actually knowing how to behave or what to say.

'Well,' she murmured at last, dropping her head to escape the deep scrutiny, 'you're engaged.'

'You thought it wouldn't happen?'

'It—it always seemed unreal. I could never quite take it in. It was a bit like being in a play, saying lines, but— but when I saw you put the ring on Cheryl's finger...'

'You felt faint.'

'It was the heat, the champagne.'

'Was it?' He tilted her chin, his fingers cool and firm against her skin, and Victoria found herself searching his face, looking for something familiar, something she had once held so dear.

It wasn't there. There was only the intent watching, the alert enquiry of a clever mind, the closed expression in dark grey eyes giving nothing away at all. She might just as well have been in court, trying to wriggle out of some hideous crime.

'I lost you long ago,' she suddenly said quietly. 'I don't really know what I'm searching for because it hasn't been there for a long, long time.' He just went on looking down at her and she gave a shuddering sigh. 'The end of an era—another end.'

'Don't, Victoria,' he said deeply. 'You lost your parents a long time ago. Don't make any sort of comparison. I'm engaged, not dead. You're just being dramatic. I cared for you while I could. Your childhood couldn't go on for ever. You're still at home and you've got Tony. What did you expect?'

'I didn't expect everything to fall apart.' She turned her face away, turned her back on him. 'That's why you made me come, isn't it? You knew I wouldn't face facts until I actually saw it happen. Nobody really needed me here. I'm superfluous, on the edge of things—not a daughter, not a sister, not anything.'

'You've always been everything in our lives!' Nick said sharply. 'You know what you meant to me, what you've always meant to me. Did you expect that to go on and on unchanging? Things do change. I changed. Live with it. This is Cheryl's day and it's important. I'm not allowing you to spoil it. I *can't* allow you to spoil it. You just don't understand.'

'*All right!*' Victoria turned brilliant blue eyes on him, eyes that were rapidly filling with tears, and then she turned away. 'Just go, Nick! Leave me alone. I can get back by myself. And don't go back and order Tony to come out here either. I can assure you that I'll come back calmly and make no sort of scene to spoil Cheryl's day.'

'I never thought you would.' He gave a sigh of regret and reached for her, pulling her back against the hard warmth of his body. 'My poor, mixed-up Victoria,' he murmured against her hair.

'I'm not mixed up.' She turned round almost defiantly, but he continued to hold her against him, looking down into her tear-wet eyes.

'You are,' he insisted softly. 'You're scared and unhappy and you don't even know why, do you?' He bent his head and kissed her forehead gently. 'Come in soon,' he urged. 'So far, nobody has missed you except Tony.'

'Then how did you know?' She wanted to hang onto him, talk to him, wipe out this day.

'I always know where you are and today I knew you would need me. Come back inside. Everything will be all right. I promise you.'

'You can't make it all right.'

'I can, Victoria. Trust me.'

He walked off across the lawn and Victoria watched him go, tall and powerful, important, and now—engaged. Tears came into her eyes again. No matter what Nick said, he could not alter things. Next time it would be his wedding. She couldn't face that. She wouldn't!

All she had to do was talk Muriel round and then take the flat. It would be easier to get out of the wedding if she lived away from home. Anyway, she couldn't face home without Nick. She knew that now. He was the prop at the centre of her life. She just could not face seeing him get married.

The dance later was just as bad as the reception had been. It was stiff, formal, with no obvious joy. She stayed with Tony for most of the time, only dancing with other people when it would have looked ill-mannered to refuse. She danced with Nick just once but he hardly spoke. He spent the time looking out over her head as if she wasn't even there.

He was mostly with Cheryl, which was natural. They seemed to spend a long time sitting together, talking quietly, obviously making plans, and Victoria watched them more often than she wanted to.

It was funny really. She had never thought them to be a well-matched couple but now they looked more relaxed in each other's company. Clearly she had missed all that before because deep down she had not expected this engagement to take place. She had been hiding her head, refusing to accept the obvious.

Nick loved Cheryl. It was clear now. Their peculiar way of carrying on was nothing really. Some people didn't show a lot of affection. The way that Nick had kissed her that last time came into her mind and she turned away abruptly, almost blundering into Lady Ashton.

'I've just been reminding Nick's mother that there will be the wedding to plan next.'

Victoria came to the present with a start to find Cheryl's mother in front of her, her eyes cold and glassy as usual.

'Er—yes. I suppose so,' she murmured. 'Muriel was speaking about it recently, complaining that she only had me to plan for.'

'Oh. You call her Muriel? It's not really surprising, I suppose. She's not your mother, after all, or so I understand.'

'No. I've just lived with them since my parents died when I was twelve,' Victoria explained, going quite pale and feeling utterly incapable of defending herself. And she knew she would have to. Lady Ashton disliked her and showed it clearly.

'Hmm. It does pose a problem, of course,' Lady Ashton mused. 'In the normal course of events, Cheryl would have wanted you to be a bridesmaid. But then, you're not Nick's sister, or anything really, are you? Perhaps Cheryl should just ask a friend. These things are so tricky, dear—the etiquette…'

She drifted away but Victoria hardly saw her. She couldn't even think of things she might have said had she been prepared for such a sly attack. She felt cold, lost, and as her eyes focused she saw Nick watching her, his gaze narrowed on her intently. What did he think she would do—rush after his future mother-in-law and knock her down?

Victoria hurried out onto the terrace and walked right to the end. It was almost ten o'clock, dusk at this time of the year, and she wished it had been winter, pitch-black. She wished she had come in her own car because she would have left right then.

Lady Ashton's remarks had been just another thing to let her know that she didn't really belong anywhere. They had also brought home to her yet again that she had lost Nick. She knew she was panicking inside, her heart fluttering like a trapped bird.

She heard footsteps, and there was nowhere to run as Nick came out and started to walk towards her. She felt utterly trapped, not in any state to face him. He said nothing until he was close but he didn't take his eyes from her.

'What did she say to you?' he asked in a dangerous voice.

'Nothing. It—it was just the normal pleasantries.'

'Victoria!' he said warningly. 'Cheryl's mother does not deal in pleasantries and she said something that made your face go pale. I've never managed to do that even when I was in a rage. So what did she say? Tell me the truth or I'll go back in there and ask her.'

'Oh, don't do that, Nick!' she said urgently. 'It really was nothing.'

'Right! I'll ask her.' He turned to leave but Victoria clutched his sleeve frantically.

'Please!' she begged.

'Then tell me, you little idiot,' he muttered, spinning to face her and pulling her against him. 'I know that viperous tongue and she's not using it on you.'

'She's going to be your mother-in-law.' Victoria reminded him in a pleading voice.

'I'll change her for a better model!' he said sarcastically, staring down at her with determined eyes. 'What did she say to you?'

'Not much, just a few words really. She was talking about the wedding.'

'And?' He tightened his grip, pulling her so close that she could hardly breathe.

'She—she pointed out that I'm not your sister and that I'm not really anything, so—so it would be wiser for Cheryl to ask a friend to be the bridesmaid, b-because of etiquette.'

'Did she?' he growled. 'Well, she's going to discover that Cheryl and I have our own plans.' His lips twisted ironically as his glance swept over her face. 'I could never have a wedding without you, princess.'

'I don't want to be a bridesmaid anyway,' she whispered, looking up at him. Her face was flushed now. And mostly it was guilt because she was luxuriating in Nick holding her close. He seemed to have forgotten to let her go and she had no inclination to wriggle free.

'Now that's tiresome,' he murmured. 'The bridegroom gets to kiss the bridesmaid. It's traditional.' He smiled down at her and Victoria could do nothing but go on looking at him. 'Your eyes are like a summer sky, huge and blue,' he said softly. 'I'll kiss you now in case you decide to back out of the wedding.'

'Don't, Nick!' She said the words in a shocked voice but she didn't attempt any escape, and it was sheer wickedness. She knew he was engaged to Cheryl but all she could think of was that at that moment he was here with her.

'Even if I thought you meant it, it wouldn't make any difference. But you don't mean it, Victoria.'

He lowered his head, finding her lips instantly, and there was nothing awkward about it. It was sweet, stinging, sharp and desperately shocking. Victoria tensed and then every bit of tautness and caution left her as his lips probed hers warmly, seeking a response, questioning her without words.

It was like floating on a cloud. She felt light, free, and her arms wanted to wind around his neck as her body softened against his.

'Nick.' She whispered his name against his mouth as he brushed his lips over hers.

'Do you think this is something you could get used to?' His eyes were laughing down at her and she felt a wave of shame at her own compliance. Nick was just amusing himself in some cruel way, behaving like the person he had become.

'Why?' she asked in a pitiful voice, and Nick's eyes narrowed at the sound. Before she could move, however, Tony erupted onto the scene.

'What the hell are you doing?' he demanded furiously.

'I'm kissing the bridesmaid.' Nick turned and stood with his arm around her and she was glad of its support. Her legs were shaking and this time she really did feel faint.

'This is *Victoria*!' Tony reminded him in an enraged voice. 'I don't care what you get up to in London, and I don't care what sort of morals these people here have, but just keep your hands off Vick!'

'For ever, I expect,' Nick said coldly as his arm fell away from her. 'I expect you want her to yourself as usual. If you want to keep her happy, however, take her home. She can't cope with anything else today. The party's over for her.'

He walked off and Victoria leaned against the wall for support. Her heart was pounding and right at that moment she felt as if she would never recover from the kiss. She was too shaken to be either shocked or ashamed now. All she could think of was the wonderful feelings that had kept bursting inside her when Nick's lips had touched hers. More than that she dared not contemplate.

'What did he do to you?' Tony asked angrily, coming to take her arm.

'Nothing, honestly,' she lied. 'He told you everything there was to tell. I—I expect he was annoyed when I told him I wouldn't go to the wedding. I think it was kiss me or shout at me, so he—he kissed me.'

It hadn't been like that and she knew it, but she had been as much to blame. She should have pushed to get free, hit him—anything. But it had been too wonderful to reject.

'He's so manipulative!' Tony snapped. 'Power certainly changed him. I'll take you home, Vick. I've had about enough of this do myself, and if I see Nick again tonight, I'll go for him.'

'He's your brother,' Victoria reminded him shakily.

'He's a swine,' Tony corrected. 'He just used his authority to subdue you in the most despicable way.'

He hadn't, and she wanted to shout it out, but there was enough trouble as it was and if Muriel and Frank found out they would be devastated. She just wanted to crawl away somewhere quiet and ask herself a few questions. They were racing through her head wildly. Why? Why had he kissed her? Why had she let him? Why was she feeling like this now?

'Let's go,' she muttered, hanging onto Tony's arm. 'Let's slip away round the back without going inside again.'

'We'd better!' Tony grated. 'I'm just about ready to tear the place apart. You were right in the first place. You shouldn't have been at this damned party—and neither should I. We're only fooling ourselves. Nick has nothing to do with us now. He behaves like a stranger and that's just about what he is.'

But he wasn't, Victoria's mind told her. He was a

warm shadow from the past, a far-off perfect knight. What he had become and why he had changed was something she could not understand. Part of her was shocked, both by his actions and her own, but part of her mourned his passing and searched constantly for the distant memories of a hero.

Nick did not come home and she knew that from now on they would see little of him. The embezzlement case was big. It was in all the papers, every one of Nick's tactics discussed and pored over, every word he uttered examined. It was just as well. If he had come home that night she would not have known how to behave and she would have looked so guilty that everyone would have guessed that something odd had happened. Tony especially would have guessed.

The incident at the party seemed to have changed Tony too, because he was not at all easygoing. He was moody, his words edged with temper, and Victoria suspected that he was about to go through one of his sullen phases. They were rare but she had seen it happen lots of times before when things had not gone according to his own plans.

'I just couldn't stand the stress he faces every day of his life,' Tony muttered at breakfast the next morning as he tossed the paper down and turned to the others. The court case and Nick's actions were splashed across the front page and Tony did not need to enlighten anyone as to the subject of his remark.

'It just washes over him,' Frank stated proudly, but Victoria glanced at Muriel and then looked away. Maybe it didn't wash over him? Nick never talked things out with anyone. He never had done. It had always been he who shouldered the burdens when they arose.

'The eldest son,' Muriel said softly, as if she were reading Victoria's mind. 'Such a lot has been expected of him always.'

'He's tough,' Tony protested curtly. 'He could always have cried on my shoulder but he never took up the opportunity.'

They laughed but it wasn't really funny. Joking was a habit with Tony, but Victoria could see the discontented look at the back of his eyes. His brush with Nick at the party seemed to have brought on a lasting fit of sulkiness.

She remembered how often she had cried on Nick's shoulder in the past, every little problem taken to him. Even yesterday at his engagement party she had been ready to cry on his shoulder. But that last kiss had changed things permanently.

Whatever Nick's intentions had been, and however he thought of it now, things were different. She wanted him. She had tried not to think about it but it was there in her head and refused to go away. He was marrying somebody else but she couldn't just let him go. He couldn't let her go either.

Eventually he would come home, of course, and then there would be trouble—because Tony would make trouble. She knew it without a single doubt. It really was time she struck out on her own. The comforting shadow had gone, and even the irritating shadow was no more. From now on Nick must be distant, out of her life.

'I'm going to try living on my own,' she announced into the silence that had fallen over the others. 'It's no use pretending that things will be the same with Nick gone. Everything changes in any family and I've decided to take the flat. I know I might not like it,' she added as Frank seemed to be about to speak, 'but it's time I tried. I'm twenty-four and most people of my age have their own place. In any case, I live a long way from work. One day I'll have to move and this flat sounds ideal.'

There was an uneasy silence but she knew they would not try to change her mind. None of them was given to

NO RISK, NO OBLIGATION TO BUY... NOW OR EVER!

CASINO JUBILEE

"Scratch'n Match" Game
Here's how to play:

1. Peel off label from front cover. Place it in the space provided opposite. With a coin carefully scratch away the silver box. This makes you eligible to receive three or more free books, and possibly another gift, depending upon what is revealed beneath the scratch-off area.

2. Send back this card and you'll receive specially selected Mills & Boon® Enchanted™ novels. These books are yours to keep absolutely free.

3. There's no catch. You're under no obligation to buy anything. We charge nothing for your first shipment. And you don't have to make any minimum number of purchases – not even one!

4. The fact is thousands of readers enjoy receiving books by mail from the Reader Service™, at least a month before they're available in the shops. They like the convenience of home delivery, and there is no extra charge for postage and packing.

5. We hope that after receiving your free books you'll want to remain a subscriber. But the choice is yours – to continue or cancel, anytime at all! So why not take up our invitation, with no risk of any kind. You'll be glad you did!

YOURS FREE!

You'll look like a million dollars when you wear this lovely necklace! Its cobra link chain is a generous 18" long and the exquisite "puffed" heart pendant completes this attractive gift.

(Pictured larger to show detail

CASINO JUBILEE
"Scratch'n Match" Game

SCRATCH HERE ?

PLACE LABEL HERE

CHECK CLAIM CHART BELOW
FOR YOUR FREE GIFTS!

N7GI

YES! I have placed my label from the front cover in the space provided above and scratched away the silver box. Please send me all the gifts for which I qualify. I understand that I am under no obligation to purchase any books, as explained on the back and on the opposite page. I am over 18 years of age.

BLOCK CAPITALS PLEASE

MS/MRS/MISS/MR _____

ADDRESS _____

_____

_____ POSTCODE _____

CASINO JUBILEE CLAIM CHART		
🍒 🍒 🍒	WORTH 4 FREE BOOKS AND A FREE NECKLACE	
🍒 🔔 🍒	WORTH 4 FREE BOOKS	
🔔 🔔 🍒	WORTH 3 FREE BOOKS	CLAIM Nº **1528**

Offer closes 31st January, 1998. We reserve the right to refuse an application. Terms and prices subject to change without notice. Offer not available for current subscribers to this series. One application per household. Offer valid in UK only. Overseas and Eire readers please write for details.

You may be mailed with offers from other reputable companies as a result of this application. If you would prefer not to share in this opportunity please tick box. ☐

MILLS & BOON IS A REGISTERED TRADE MARK OF HARLEQUIN MILLS & BOON LIMITED.

◆ DETACH AND POST CARD TODAY! ◆

THE READER SERVICE™: HERE'S HOW IT WORKS

Accepting free books puts you under no obligation to buy anything. You may keep the books and gift and return the despatch note marked "cancel". If we don't hear from you, about a month later we will send you 6 brand new Mills & Boon Enchanted novels and invoice you for just £2.20* each. That's the complete price – there is no extra charge for postage and packing. You may cancel at any time, otherwise every month we'll send you six more books, which you may either purchase or return - the choice is yours.

The Reader Service™
FREEPOST
Croydon
Surrey
CR9 3WZ

NO
STAMP
NEEDED

If offer card is missing, write to: The Reader Service, P.O. Box 236, Croydon, Surrey CR9 3RU.

issuing orders. They had always left that to Nick and now he was no longer here.

'I'll come and look it over with you,' Tony announced gruffly later on, but Victoria shook her head.

'On my own, Tony,' she insisted. 'If I make a mistake I want it to be my own mistake. I'm a different person at work and I'm quite tired of living two lives.'

'Nick,' Tony surmised angrily. 'He would never let you grow up and take risks.' He gave her a sharp look. 'I don't suppose you'd like to place a bet about this?'

'What do you mean?'

'You know what I mean. When he hears about it there'll be hell to pay.'

'He's engaged. Soon he'll be married. It has nothing to do with Nick. He'll be living his own life.'

'But he'll not let you go all the same. He *can't* let you go. He'll still be keeping a grip on you when you're sixty.'

'Don't be ridiculous!' Victoria snapped. 'He won't have either the time or the inclination to interfere.'

'We'll see.'

Tony let the subject drop but it left Victoria feeling under pressure, as if she had to act right now, this minute, and Tony's moods were getting on her nerves. It really was time she left because at the moment she felt a little like a bone being fought over by two quite ferocious dogs. Tony liked all his own way and Nick had become out of bounds for her.

Besides, when he did come back she didn't quite know how she would behave. She didn't know how she would look at him, how he would look at her. They seemed to have a guilty secret that was far bigger than the kiss Tony had witnessed.

She brought up the matter of the flat at once when she went in to work the following day and Greg's face lit up.

'We'll look at it over during the lunch hour,' he promised. 'You're being very wise. It's time you left home.'

That had a very ominous ring and Victoria had to
think hard about the advantages of living in London. She
had thought it all out before—told herself she would be
going home every weekend, reminded herself about the
awful drive to work—but now, faced with it, she could
only think about home.

She would miss Tony, in spite of his recent moods.
In any case, the mood wouldn't last. She had seen it all
before. She knew he expected her to back out of moving
at the last minute, though, and it was that thought that
drove her on.

The flat seemed to be very small after the size of
Clifford Court, and Victoria walked from room to room
as Greg watched.

'It's a nice place,' he insisted as he saw the dubious
look on her face. 'Good view.'

'If you like streets and traffic,' Victoria muttered,
looking out of the window. It wasn't quite what she had
envisaged. She had never lived in a flat but she had been
inside Nick's. It was luxurious and looked out over a
green park.

She mentioned this to Greg and he grinned widely.

'Have you any idea at all about the sort of money
Nick King makes?' he chuckled. 'In some ways you're
quite unworldly, Victoria. Your adoptive brother, or
whatever he is, makes a great deal of money. Affording
a luxurious flat is no problem to him. Besides, this is
close to work and I live in the same block.'

'That's nice,' Victoria said with slightly forced cheer-
fulness. 'I'll be able to get to know your wife.'

He didn't say anything, but she was too taken with
wondering what Tony would think of the flat to pay

much attention. She could hardly refuse to allow him to look round the place. He was her lifelong friend. All the same, she would wait until his present fit of angry gloom departed. She glanced at Greg and gave a resigned sigh.

'If I'm going to take the plunge I may as well take it now,' she said.

'Snap it up while you can,' he agreed eagerly. 'Strike while the iron's hot.'

It was much more like act while the power in her life was otherwise occupied as far as Victoria was concerned, and Tony's words came back to her with an ominous ring... 'There'll be hell to pay.'

Deep inside, she knew he was right.

CHAPTER SIX

IT WAS a week before she had the flat signed for and, behaving quite out of character, Victoria just kept silent until then. Better to present everyone with a *fait accompli* than enter into any further and useless discussions. She told Muriel and Frank one evening before Tony arrived home from work, and after a long pause of disappointment they both questioned her enthusiastically.

'Is it furnished?' Frank wanted to know, and Victoria grimaced.

'Basic—very basic,' she admitted, and that was quite enough to have them planning to come to London and help her to set things up properly.

'Don't think we're interfering, Victoria,' Muriel pleaded. 'It's what we would have done for our own daughter, if we had had one.'

'I know,' Victoria soothed, 'and you're not interfering. I've neither the time nor the—'

'Money?' Frank interrupted with a grin. 'If you've got the key, we'll come tomorrow. We'll discuss it and get started right away.'

It left her feeling happy, and it had certainly taken Muriel's mind off the fact that she was about to leave home. They agreed to meet at her flat the next day after work and then have a meal together in town.

Strangely, nothing was mentioned to Tony when he came home, and after some deep consideration Victoria decided to tell him herself. His petulant mood seemed to have passed and she wanted to keep things as normal as possible.

'Do I get invited?' he asked when she told him about her plans.

'Whenever you like. Just walk in any time.' Victoria smiled cheerfully at him and he sat opposite, looking thoughtful.

'Funny,' he mused, 'out of the blue everything is broken up, finished.'

'It's the normal thing,' she said quickly. 'People go off in different directions but they don't necessarily grow apart. I'll be here at weekends and every single holiday I get, because basically I live here.'

'Then why don't you stay here?' Tony enquired moodily. 'I'm not fooled by this travel to work thing, Vick. I know why you're leaving. It's Nick. You can't face him, can you?'

'I have faced him,' she reminded him quietly. 'I've faced him for about three years. So has everyone else for that matter.'

'But not in the way you'll have to face him now,' he pointed out. He looked up at her levelly. 'You were coping quite well with his irascibility—until he got engaged.'

'Rubbish!' Victoria scoffed. 'What difference could that have made?'

'Before his engagement there was always a possibility that things would return to the comfortable norm,' Tony reminded her. 'Now there's no chance at all. He's pushed you out into the cold, hard world so you're fleeing the nest.'

'You're probably a very good solicitor,' Victoria managed mockingly. 'You're not a good detective, though. I do hope you'll hire one if the need arises.'

'Oh, I'm not looking into Nick's motives,' he said drily, 'just yours. I know without any detective work what *he'll* do. He'll come after you and drag you back here. So you see, I can afford to sit and wait magnanimously.'

Victoria's face went red and he looked at her with smug assurance.

'The past is finished,' she snapped. 'He's gone.'

'But not forgotten.' Tony gave her a calculating look. 'He's clever, Vick, more than a match for the likes of us. Do you ever know what Nick is thinking? Do you ever catch even a glimpse of it in his eyes?'

'I really don't care what he's thinking,' she assured him haughtily. 'I'll do exactly as I like.'

'I know,' Tony murmured. 'You always have done— if Nick liked it too. That's the way it's always been. What makes you imagine it's changed?'

'He's engaged, left, gone, vanished!' she pointed out hotly.

'He'll never be gone,' Tony muttered. In any case, you couldn't manage without him, could you?' He stood and gave her a slightly sarcastic smile. 'Goodnight, Vick. I'll see you tomorrow. I'll have to get you a flat-warming present.'

'Thank you! I'll take the well-sharpened axe, if you don't mind. I can see I'm going to need one.'

He laughed and went out of the room, quite back to normal. And what was normal? Victoria asked herself crossly. Tony's mutterings were a bit too close to the mark. She had always done exactly as she liked—with Nick's permission.

'Abominations!' she said aloud. 'He's changed, gone away, and that's exactly what I'm going to do.'

The following day, Victoria could see immediately that Muriel and Frank were not too impressed by the flat. They stood in silence and looked round with the same dubious expression on their faces that she had felt on her own when she had first seen it.

'Not exactly fabulous, hmm?' she asked with a wry look at Muriel.

'Well—it could have possibilities,' Muriel murmured doubtfully.

'There's the possibility that you'll not settle here,' Frank pointed out with a grin. 'Therefore, I approve of it. You two girls work out what's needed and we'll get to the shops. Meanwhile, I'll make a cup of tea for all of us.'

'Er—no cups, no kettle,' Victoria said ruefully.

'So you're not really fixed on the idea of the flat?' He was laughing, and Muriel looked at him firmly.

'She hasn't even left home yet. In any case, where would Victoria get cups and kettles or anything else? This is her first venture into the business of living away.' She looked at Victoria a little warily. 'You know there are a lot of your parents' things in store for you?'

'I don't want them yet. When I have a house of my own, when I really leave home...'

'When you're married,' Muriel finished gently. 'I know, dear. What we need now are bits and pieces to brighten this place up. I'll make a list.'

Making lists had always been Muriel's delight and Victoria smiled at Frank. They both knew that Muriel would take over and it suited Victoria well enough. This flat was not going to be a home and she wondered a little anxiously just what it was going to be. Another bolt-hole like her cupboard in the storm? What was she escaping from this time? She didn't really have to dig any deeper because she knew. Nick. Always it was Nick, the phantom picture in the corner of her mind.

Brightening up the flat took a week, because they could only go to the shops when Victoria had finished at work, and she was astounded at the number of things she actually needed badly and could not manage without. She hadn't even given thought to the bedding, and Muriel would not countenance the curtains that were draped depressingly at the windows.

The procedure was exciting, though, and served to take her mind off other things, and Tony was too busy to interfere. She knew it was giving Muriel and Frank a stake in her new life. It even brought them closer together, and by the time she was ready to move in they were both quite happily resigned to it.

All the same, she couldn't bring herself to remove all her clothes from Clifford Court and Frank noted this with one of his wry grins. She wasn't really leaving home and he knew it. She was camping out, escaping, and Victoria hoped he didn't get around to fathoming out exactly why.

In the middle of the following week, Tony called round with a bottle of wine and invited himself for a meal. He sat in the kitchen as Victoria cooked it and he brought up the subject of Nick almost at once.

'It looks as if he's got that crook, Kenton, in a stranglehold,' he said, and Victoria nodded.

'I know. It was on the news.' The cameras had caught Nick leaving the court but he had simply ignored the media. He had looked grim and Victoria had thought he looked stressed, overworked. 'He looked tense,' she muttered.

'It's the size of this case. He's never lost yet. That's why he's always in so much demand. Using your brain like that must be a bit sapping on the energy. He hasn't rung home, though, so he doesn't know about *you* yet. Let's hope he remains in blissful ignorance of your flight until this case is over.'

'Moving here was not flight,' Victoria pointed out stiffly, 'and it has nothing to do with Nick, so don't start on again, Tony.'

'But I'm not,' he protested. 'I'm telling you that the

coast is clear for now. This is the longest time he's ever been before getting in touch with home. I'm wondering if it's the case. I think he's taking the threats from the underworld more seriously than he admits. He wouldn't want to bring that home. He's used to dealing with things himself and not putting his family at risk.'

'You don't seriously think that?' Victoria looked at him in near horror. He said it was no different from any other time.'

'I think it is, though. The papers are full of this Kenton's past and his associates.'

'They make a lot out of anything,' Victoria insisted, too scared for Nick to allow herself to believe any of this. 'He's away because he's engaged. He'll be giving Cheryl all his spare time.'

'She's in Paris,' Tony murmured wryly. 'She sneaked off all by herself. Unfortunately there was one of those pushy photographers at the airport. He spotted her. It was in the paper the other day, after a report about the trial. The gist of it was that the new fiancée was getting out of the limelight for when the trial ends. She looked hopping mad when she was spotted.'

'Cheryl?' Victoria asked in some amazement. It was difficult to imagine Cheryl Ashton being hopping mad or even slightly displeased.

'The very one,' Tony pronounced with comfortable satisfaction. 'So, you see, Nick's not spending his off-duty minutes with his beloved. He's just keeping clear of Clifford Court.'

'I wonder why?' Victoria mused.

'I've told you what I think. I know you're too scared for him to even consider it but it has to be faced. Or maybe he's ashamed of his actions at the party,' Tony added a trifle sharply. 'He kissed you. Perhaps he's now filled with remorse about his fit of temper.'

'This food may end up on your head!' Victoria

warned, hoping that her flushed cheeks would be put down to the heat of the cooker or her ready temper.

'Just musing,' Tony said, holding up his hands in surrender.

Just prying, she suspected. And there was no mystery about Nick. He was busy. The mystery was Cheryl, although she might really just be escaping the limelight, as the paper had apparently surmised. Victoria was quite astonished that Cheryl had had the courage to go off completely alone. Living with parents like hers was a good way of draining the courage out of anyone, and Cheryl could not stand up to any sort of attack from them. She was quite sure about that.

Tony left at about nine o'clock, and almost immediately afterwards Craig knocked on the door. He looked a bit sheepish when Victoria answered.

'I thought I'd just pop round and see how you've settled,' he told her. 'I didn't come earlier because I knew you had company.'

'Tony,' she said, annoyed at the idea that he had been spying on her. 'He's Nick's brother.'

'Another King,' Craig acknowledged uneasily. 'Another one full of power?'

She had to smile at the thought of Tony being full of power and it relaxed her rather stiff attitude.

'Come in,' she invited. 'Tony's my lifelong friend and he's not a bit like Nick. I can't see Tony ever making the headlines.'

She made coffee again and Craig seemed set to stay for ages. Victoria frowned to herself. She hadn't thought of this when she had decided to move in here. She felt uncomfortable about him being here when his wife was probably waiting in their own flat and getting annoyed.

'Why didn't you bring your wife?' she enquired. 'I was hoping to get to know her.'

'She's not actually here,' Craig said edgily. 'In fact, we're trying a separation.'

Victoria just stared at him. Of course, it was none of her business, but she had mentioned getting to know his wife when he had shown her round the flat at first. Come to think of it, he had never answered.

'Why didn't you tell me before?' she asked quietly, and his edginess turned to downright discomfort.

'I thought you might not take the flat,' he confessed. 'I knew you wanted it and I thought you might back off if you knew I was alone here.'

'Why should I? You're my boss,' she pointed out. All the same, her heart sank a little. If Craig was having marital problems he would be wanting to talk, and she had not come here to be a marriage guidance counsellor.

'I thought we might go out together occasionally,' Craig suggested, looking a little more relaxed at her attitude.

'To make your wife jealous?' Victoria asked astutely. 'No, thank you, sir. If I want to be in trouble I can make plenty for myself without assistance.'

'I'd really like to go out with you, Victoria,' he told her earnestly, and she stood, smiling down at him quizzically, perfectly in control of the situation.

'No,' she said firmly. 'We get on well at work. You're the boss and I like that relationship.'

'OK. I can take a hint.' He stood too, and prepared to leave. 'I expect your heart's given to someone else, a beautiful girl like you.'

'My heart is sealed in plastic,' Victoria assured him. 'Don't bother yourself about its condition.'

She edged him to the door. At this rate she just might need that axe. It was obvious how his mind was working and she hoped he would not make a habit of this sort of thing.

She smiled him out of the flat and shut the door firmly,

leaning against it, quite shaken by this unusual turn of events. How quaint he was really. Her heart 'given to someone else'. She grinned to herself and felt absolutely furious when Nick's face came into her mind. It was time she cleared out the ever-present shadow that prowled through her head.

She hadn't even gathered up the cups when there was another knock on the door, and this time she felt really cross. It was ten o'clock, work in the morning, and she still had to do the dishes. Tony's affection did not stretch to doing pots and pans. If Craig had thought of something to tell her he could have left it until morning, and if he was coming back to try his luck again...!

She wrenched the door open in a fit of annoyance and she could feel her skin go hot and then cold when she found herself looking up into two dark grey eyes that held a good deal more annoyance than her own. This was it and she knew it. She could not go on like this with Nick. She had to face him down and get on with her own life.

She threw the door wide open.

'Come in,' she invited sarcastically. 'There's nothing like a steady stream of visitors to make one feel popular. Tony came for dinner, Craig came for coffee and now you, the great man himself. I'm overwhelmed.'

Nick came in and shut the door with rather frightening quiet. He looked too big for the flat, too tall, too important and certainly too elegant. Idiotic things began to run through her mind. She was glad the curtains had been changed. She was glad the kitchen door was closed and he couldn't see the havoc that making dinner had wrought. How had he found her and why had he bothered? It all scrambled up in her mind, making her nervous, jumpy, and when she spoke all the wrong words came out.

'What do you want?'

His dark brows rose and he stood looking at her coolly.

'If that's how you greet your guests, your popularity won't last long,' he assured her sardonically.

'I—I didn't mean to say it like that,' she muttered in confusion. 'You startled me. I didn't expect you to...'

'Of course you did,' he corrected softly. 'You knew perfectly well that I'd be here the moment I knew about this. I imagined that the problem had been solved quite a while ago. As I remember you changed your mind when you saw how upset everyone was.'

'They're not upset now,' she insisted, still watching him warily. 'Would you like to sit down?'

'Not particularly.' He put his hands in his pockets and began to walk around the room, looking as if he was making mental notes of everything.

He was prowling, just like he prowled in her mind, and Victoria knew that anything she said just then would sound either foolish or scared. She wasn't scared. She told herself that fact very firmly but it didn't stop her legs from shaking a bit.

Nick was danger. Even Craig had seemed more likely in this place. She had definitely had the upper hand with him—and with Tony. With Nick she was always on the defensive.

'I'll make some coffee,' she announced breathlessly, but he didn't look round at her.

'Tea,' he said quietly, and she just dived into the kitchen and stared in near horror at the chaos there. It was ridiculous! She was acting as if Nick were some sort of inspector. He couldn't even come into the kitchen unless she invited him in. This was *her* place.

There was another knock on the door and Nick answered it before she could even take two strides.

'Victoria. I never meant...' It was Craig, and his voice trailed away at the sight of Nick standing tall and icily interested at the door. 'Oh, it's you. I—er—thought it was Victoria. I'll go,' Craig finished uneasily.

'Do that,' Nick advised coldly, and closed the door as Victoria burst into the small sitting room in a fury.

'How dare you see off my guests in such an uncouth manner?' she stormed. 'You have no right to even answer the door. This is my flat!'

'Uncouth?' Nick was obviously running the word through his mind as he stood and regarded her ironically. 'An interesting word, quite new. I've never been called that before.'

'I don't expect you've ever behaved like that before,' Victoria raged. 'It's just with me, isn't it? You imagine you're my keeper, my master, my general supervisor!'

'Bring the tea,' he ordered in amused resignation as he sat down and made himself at home. 'I thought I was doing you a favour in seeing him off. You told me he'd already been here once tonight. Did he want to borrow something? A cup of sugar?'

'He's my boss,' Victoria stated firmly, wondering if Nick could possibly know about Craig's break-up with his wife. How could he, unless he was reading her mind? She went back for the tea, hoping the subject would be changed when she went back in. And why hadn't she ordered Nick out of the flat anyway? The answer depressed her considerably. She didn't want to, that was why.

'Well, this is cosy,' Nick remarked smoothly as he sat back and drank his tea. It wasn't what he meant at all and she knew it. Victoria perched on the edge of the other armchair and gathered her strength for the expected attack.

'Tony said you hadn't called home at all,' she managed quietly. 'How did you know I was here?'

'I telephoned this evening. Mother told me. She was, to my surprise, full of enthusiasm. The reason became clear when she told me you'd let her plan all the additions to the flat.' He looked across at her. 'Clever girl. You're learning fast.'

'She wanted to,' Victoria protested, 'and it made her feel better, more part of things.'

'It would,' he agreed. 'And how does Tony fit into the picture? Does he feel part of "things"? Is he angry that you've left home or is he glad to be able to come here and have you all to himself. Are you planning to share this place?'

'We are not!' Victoria stated hotly. 'This is my own flat. Anyway,' she added firmly, 'it's a one-bedroom flat.'

'Does Parker appreciate that fact, or does he think it's a good thing anyway?'

'I told you! He's married!' Victoria snapped.

She was well aware that she was the only one showing any obvious annoyance. Nick's voice was quite calm, almost casual, but it didn't fool her at all. He was winding her up for the kill. She'd seen him do it in court when she was much younger and she had wondered then why he was being so relaxed—until he had suddenly pounced.

'Of course he is. So he came for coffee with his wife?'

There it was, and she actually had few choices. She could stay silent and condemn herself, or answer and condemn herself, or she could tell him to mind his own business.

'She wasn't at home,' Victoria hedged, adding for good measure, 'Not that it has anything to do with you.'

'Mrs Parker was having an evening out with her friends,' he surmised, 'and Mr Parker was having coffee with *his* friend. How wonderfully mature and modern.'

'They're separated,' Victoria said, with more resignation in her voice than she realised. Lying to Nick was impossible. It had always been impossible.

'So now he wants you,' Nick stated very, very quietly. 'Is he prepared to fight Tony for you? Or is Tony ignorant of this exciting undercurrent?'

'You're speaking to me as if I'm a—a temptress!' Victoria choked, standing up in her agitation.

'A siren?' he enquired lazily. 'Not really. You've stepped in at the deep end and I just want you to understand about the big fish at the bottom of the pool.'

'Tony is my friend,' she protested, almost tearfully, 'and Craig is my boss, and you have no right...'

'No right to protect you? I'll never surrender that right, princess.'

'You're engaged! Leave me alone!' She was almost at the stage of wringing her hands and Nick slowly stood, putting his cup down and then looking at her seriously.

'I can't leave you alone,' he assured her softly. 'I'll never want to. Cheryl and I are engaged for—mutual protection. It's an arrangement.'

'So is every engagement. People arrange to get engaged.' Victoria knew she was whispering, and staring at Nick as if he were mad.

He made a wry face. 'I doubt if many engagements are like ours.' He walked across to her and stood looking down into her face. 'Stop pretending that I scare you, Victoria,' he said quietly. 'We both know that your own feelings are scaring you.' He linked his arms loosely around her waist, and just as she thought he was going to kiss her again he glanced thoughtfully around the flat. 'Maybe you're better off here,' he mused. 'It's pretty secure and not many people know you're here. See that you keep a low profile.'

'Why?' There was a degree of seriousness in his voice that scared her all over again, and Victoria gazed up at him earnestly.

'I want you to be safe—and I'm not talking about

your amorous boss. He's merely a temporary nuisance.'
Nick fixed her with dark grey eyes. 'He annoys me,
though. Keep him strictly in his place.'

'You haven't got anything to do with me...' she
began, but he stopped the words with warm lips just
when she didn't expect it.

'I have everything to do with you and you know it,'
he whispered in her ear. 'You may be the apple of
Tony's eye, the cream in his coffee, but I'll always be
there, Victoria.'

Next day Victoria went to work feeling dazed and depressed. There was a sort of awe lingering in her mind
after her encounter with Nick. She was puzzled, scared.
He had spoken so oddly about his engagement, as if it
was a passing thing, and he had made it quite clear that
he would always be in her life.

Always was a long time, especially if he didn't belong
to her. And he didn't belong to her. He never would.
The awe that lingered came from his final words—'I'll
always be there, Victoria.'

The words might have been quietly spoken but they
had carried so much conviction, so much power, that she
didn't doubt them. Like it or not, Nick was her shadow
for the rest of her days, and, dramatic though it might
seem, she believed him. She would never even be able
to begin to learn to live without him but he would always
be distant, appearing when he thought best, leaving as
he had left the night before and getting on with his own
life.

Since the engagement party she was different, and
well aware of it. The anger and frustration had gone and
with it had gone her peace of mind—because now she
was attached to Nick in a completely different way. She
was restless and unhappy and she had no idea what to
do about it.

Craig called her into his office, glancing at her a little warily when she stood there looking downcast.

'If I upset you last night...' he began, but Victoria managed a weak smile and shook her head.

'You didn't. Forget it.'

'He looked angry.' Craig stared at her glumly and she felt her cheeks beginning to flush.

'Nick? Don't worry about it. He was a little off with me too. I think he's tired with this case he's prosecuting.'

'Not surprising,' Craig agreed. 'It's a big scene he's playing and there's too much media attention. There's the personal risk he's taking too.'

'Do you think so?' Victoria bit her lip and stared at him anxiously. Even Tony, with his flip attitude to life, was convinced there was a risk.

'I hate to scare you but I do think so. They may have Kenton in jail but they haven't got anyone else. Who knows what they'll do? They'll be scared that Kenton will talk and drag others into this. On the other hand, only someone like Nick King could nail him so securely to the mast. They may decide that it would be wiser to have King out of the way.'

He stopped when he saw her pale face.

'Pay no attention,' he urged quickly. 'I'm being dramatic. Nothing like that happens in my life. It's such a big thrill actually knowing the man involved. I'm sure someone like Nick King will have thought out everything.'

Victoria nodded and turned to the door. He had. He had thought out that she might be in danger too, which was ridiculous. Why should she be? She had never figured hugely in Nick's public life. She didn't figure in it at all now. Maybe Cheryl was in danger? Maybe that was why she had shot off to Paris?

Anyway, that seemed to be Craig's embarrassment

sorted out, his conscience cleared and his feathers smoothed. She wished she could do the same thing for herself. She seemed to be walking about in a dream, with Nick's face in front of her all the time.

'I didn't call you in here to discuss that, actually,' Craig pointed out when she was clearly about to walk off. 'I've had a big meeting with Alfred.'

'I thought you could manage without his help now,' Victoria said quickly, walking back to his desk. What was about to happen? Surely Craig wasn't about to tell her that his brother wanted to get rid of her? It would be the final straw.

'I *can* manage without his help,' Craig agreed. 'Whether I want to or not is another matter. He's willing to keep his money in the business to allow us to expand. He's even been probing a market for us.'

Victoria came back and sat down. This was most interesting because she knew that Alfred Parker thought advertising was somehow shoddy, almost immoral. It managed to get Nick out of her mind for a minute.

'I thought he disapproved of the business?' she asked, and Craig gave his first grin.

'He never disapproves of money. He's impressed. I showed him the accounts, the letter of praise from the bank, and offered to pay him back with interest. He became quite agitated.'

'Do go on,' Victoria invited. Alfred Parker was as cold as a fish on a slab. Agitated was a word that did not fit him at all.

'He seems to have had a change of heart,' Craig murmured, leaning back in his chair and beaming at her. 'I think he can smell money now and he's sticking in there. I've mulled it over and I think it suits us to keep his cash. He's been putting feelers out in Scotland. He owns a place up there. I want you to go and follow up his leads.'

'*Not*, if I have to stay with your brother and his wife,' Victoria said strongly. 'Why can't you go yourself anyway?'

'I have to hang around here,' Craig muttered uncomfortably. 'There's Mary. She might just change her mind. If she comes back and I'm away…' He looked up at her. 'I'm sorry about last night, you know. I was a bit low in spirits.'

'Forget it,' Victoria said. 'I've told you that already. We all have our fits of madness.' And she should know. Hadn't it been a fit of madness each time Nick had kissed her? Hadn't it been a fit of madness each time she had stood there and let him? And wasn't she mad now, worrying about some nebulous future when Nick would suddenly appear and rock her world?

'I'll go up to Scotland,' she offered cheerfully. 'Always providing that your brother does not insist on going with me to spy.'

'Mary and I have a cottage up there too,' Craig said. 'It's just north of Edinburgh. You can stay at the cottage and drive to all the places he's mapped out. It will be a little holiday for you, make up for your hard work and my clumsiness last night.'

Victoria gave him an ironic look. Getting new business would be no holiday, and if she failed Alfred Parker would say she was incompetent. Still, she could stay on afterwards for a weekend and have a break. She certainly needed one. More than that, though, she could get away.

'If we finally decide to open an office in Edinburgh, can I…?' she began eagerly, thinking of the distance from London and Nick.

'Victoria, *please*!' Craig laughed. 'You're not going off to distant parts permanently. You make this place work and that is the nub of things. Anyway, I don't like the boat rocking. If we get a lot of business up there you'll end up doing plenty of travelling, but as to a permanent move—to use your own sweet words, forget it.'

Well, it had been worth a try, and Victoria went back to her office with more to think about than Nick and his strange and overwhelming ways. She would make this trip last as long as possible. Perhaps when she came back she would feel differently. Something had to change and it would not be Nick.

To her amusement, Muriel was more excited about it than she was herself.

'You're getting to be quite important, Victoria,' she said eagerly when Victoria went home for the weekend. 'Just think of it, that big account and now travelling for the firm. I used to feel that Nick would never let you grow up. He liked you just as you were. I don't believe he's taken too well to you going out into the world of big business. He'll have to adjust his thinking.'

Victoria didn't know what to say. All she could do was mumble and smile foolishly. Why, oh, why did her life revolve around Nick? And why did everyone expect that to be all right? Everyone except Tony.

'Mother is probably the most naïve person in the world,' he announced as his mother left the room. 'She still thinks you're a golden-haired child and under Nick's wing.'

'I expect it's more comfortable for her to think like that,' Victoria murmured uneasily. 'I imagine mothers like people to stay young.'

'That may be true but she's proud of your new importance. Nick is the one with the problem. He's had the problem ever since you came back from university. You came back with a mind of your own and he didn't like it.'

'Why do we always have to talk about Nick?' Victoria snapped impatiently. 'Anyone would think he was the only person in the world.'

'Isn't he?' Tony asked, giving her a calculating look. 'You're having a lot of trouble shrugging him off, Vick. You don't exactly know where he fits into your life now, do you?'

'He doesn't fit into my life at all,' Victoria protested. 'I haven't been close to Nick for years and you know it.'

'Things change,' Tony reminded her. 'You said that yourself. It's what they change into that matters.'

He seemed determined to pry and Victoria had one last go at stopping him.

'I'm trying to wangle my way into being in charge of the Edinburgh office if we open one,' she told him, changing the subject and putting out of her mind Craig's flat refusal on that point.

'OK. I'll let Nick know,' Tony assured her in a smoothly off-hand manner, the calculating look still there. 'It won't alter things—apart from the fact that he'll be furious.'

'You're getting to be as big a nuisance as he is,' Victoria pointed out angrily, and he gave her one of his wry grins.

'In an entirely different way, though,' he assured her. 'I'm your bosom pal. I wonder what Nick is?'

Victoria walked out huffily because she had wondered just that herself. Sometimes Nick seemed to be a distant dream, sometimes an ever-present part of her conscience. And sometimes he seemed like her destiny.

CHAPTER SEVEN

CRAIG insisted that she went by train to Edinburgh and arranged for her to pick up a hire car once she was there. It gave her a much needed rest and it was only as she sat back, watching the countryside flash by, that Victoria realised how tired and stressed she had become these past few weeks.

She had not been able to get Nick out of her mind for more than a minute each day, and now she was carrying a huge burden of guilt about the kisses. She had been left feeling bewildered, pulled in many directions, and the only sensible thing to do was get far away. Well, Edinburgh should be far enough, although it didn't really matter where she went, so long as it was a safe distance from London.

The car was waiting for her when she arrived at the station in Edinburgh, all very slickly arranged as Craig had promised, but it was small and not new by any means. Victoria eyed it with a frown. If she was to drive up to some place to make an impression and get new business, this was not the way to go about it. She would have to park elsewhere and arrive on foot. All she could hope for was that the car was reliable. She would speak severely to Craig about this frugal attitude. It had the ring of his brother about it.

The engine sounded quite sweet, however, and she nodded cheerfully to the man who had delivered it and drove off, highly amused when he looked embarrassed that this elegantly dressed young lady should have to get into a rather inferior car. If he thought it, then what would prospective clients think? It was a good point to make to Craig and she drove along quite happily, turning over in her mind exactly what she would say to him.

Craig's cottage was north of Edinburgh, and when she consulted the map and realised just how far north, Victoria understood that both the car and the cottage were part of the same frugal plan. It would have been better to stay in some hotel in the city and get to the clients from there, but of course that would have cost money. This way she was staying in Scotland for nothing *and* buying her own food. She would see to it that Craig picked up the bills.

The weather was hot and sticky, and as she drove along with the windows wound down Victoria appreciated the beauty of the countryside. There was so little traffic, so much space and beauty that she felt her spirits lifting with every mile and her annoyance at Craig's penny-pinching ways fading. If the cottage was half reasonable she would stay up here for a few days when she had finished. London could manage without her. It was ages since she had taken a holiday. She put her problems right to the back of her mind and settled down to enjoying everything. She would forget all about Nick.

An hour later she saw the landmark she had been looking for: the soft, rounded heights of the Ochil Hills. Victoria stopped the car and smiled at the sight. It was so beautiful. There were sheep grazing far up, tiny, white and fluffy from this distance, and at the sound of a waterfall she got out of the car to gaze over the rails at the side of the road and watch the water glittering in the sun. It was all clean and clear, giant ferns growing by the water with wet, mossy rocks catching the gleam of the sunlight.

'This is the life,' Victoria muttered to herself, narrowing her eyes against the brightness. It wasn't really, though, and she knew it. She felt alone, unhappy, almost a different person, and she knew that her loneliness was due to the fact that there was no way that Nick could suddenly appear. She had slipped away without him knowing anything and now her mind was searching for him, wanting him to come, wanting to go back.

She frowned into the falling water. It had always been Nick. He had given her confidence in the first place. It had been Nick who had rebuilt her life and made her whole again. Now she was letting her feelings for him destroy her. He belonged to Cheryl.

She got back into the car and drove on, all her attention now given to finding her way, and soon she came to the tiny village that Craig had mentioned, Arna Glen. There were a couple of shops and one tiny inn that was closed, but it was a weather-beaten old man directed her.

'The cottage?' he mused as she enquired. 'Aye. Two miles up this road and then down the lane. Ye'll no miss it. The Englishman put a sign up.'

He looked pretty disgusted, and Victoria wondered what Craig had done to bring this disdain upon his head. She found out soon enough when she drove on and saw the sign. The old man had been right; she couldn't miss it. It was a large white board, surrounded by shocking black wrought-iron, and the stark black lettering proclaimed 'Mary's Dell'.

It was utterly incongruous in this soft, sweeping countryside and Victoria's face lit up in a grin. She was quite sure that Mary Parker had not requested this and she rather suspected that Craig had been up here since their separation and created this monstrosity in a fit of melancholy. No doubt when they got back together again he would be ordered to take it down at once.

There was Mary's touch in the cottage, though, and Victoria was very pleasantly surprised. It had been skilfully modernised and the tiny sitting room had lovely blue and white covers on the settee and armchairs. There was a dark polished table and chairs in the same room and a bookcase filled with bright paperbacks. No television and no telephone—exactly what she wanted. It was a comfortable bolt-hole, away from the world, and she brought her things in from the car and then explored the rest of the place.

It didn't take much doing. There was a kitchen across the passage and upstairs a bedroom and bathroom. She settled in and then drove to the shops in the village to stock up with supplies. Tomorrow was work but for now she could rest, safe from intrusion. There was no Muriel to worry about her, no Tony to jolt her conscience and no Nick. Nick was far away.

To her great astonishment, tears filled her eyes at the thought, but she brushed them away impatiently. Nick was gone. Her feelings were just a lingering dream from the past.

Next morning, Victoria woke up feeling tremendously rested. The quiet of the place had been total. The world had seemed to contain nothing but herself and one owl last night, and she sang in the shower and ate more breakfast than usual. Today she was filled with drive and energy and as she went out into the morning sunshine and opened the car she took a deep, satisfying breath and prepared to set off.

'Look out, Edinburgh, here I come!' she announced into the miraculous silence. She was back to normal, and although far at the back of her mind Nick still waited, he didn't worry her and he didn't make her feel sad. There was something quite wonderful about him and she loved him. She could admit that without fear. He seemed to be all around her.

The knowledge gave her an inner glow and she knew that all day she was impressing people. The peculiar happiness radiated from her as if she had a charmed life.

Later in the week, after two trips to Glasgow and a

follow-up call to the Edinburgh contacts, Victoria found her jobs finished. It was Thursday afternoon and her long weekend was assured. The weather was unnaturally hot and for the rest of the time she intended to simply laze about in the cottage garden. On Sunday evening she would drive back to the station and catch the train home.

A quick glance at the fridge told her that she would have to do some more shopping if she wished to simply stay and rest but, faced with it, Victoria could not bring herself to get back into a hot car. Even at this time of day the sky was brazen, and the build-up of heat over the last few days had brought about an almost explosive feeling in the air. She decided to stroll down to the village shops before they closed so she put on a flimsy cotton dress, a mere slip of a garment that left her shoulders bare and cool. With a straw sun hat and flat sandals she felt ready for the walk and set off quite eagerly.

When she started back with her shopping, the idea of a walk did not seem to be so sound because a strong breeze had sprung up from nowhere, and looking back from the village she saw a peculiar mist forming over the rounded outlines of the Ochil Hills.

'It's rain,' a woman who was hurrying from the shop at the same time told her. 'You can always see it over the hills before it gets here. Just about long enough time to bring in the washing.'

But not long enough to walk two miles to the cottage and get down the lane, Victoria assessed. It was still too hot to run and in any case she had the shopping. She submitted to the idea of getting a soaking and set off resolutely.

The rain caught her when she was about half a mile from the turn into the lane and it was an unbelievable torrent. Out of what had appeared to be a clear sky the deluge came with a sort of surreal force that had her ducking her head and sometimes closing her eyes. The heat left her skin, and by the time she turned into the lane she was shivering and soaked. Her dress was sticking to her, clinging around her legs, and her beautiful straw hat was flapping around her face, heavy with water that ran onto her shoulders in a steady stream.

The lane seemed to be never-ending, and by the time the cottage appeared Victoria had long since stopped looking ahead. The only way to make any progress was to watch her wet feet and tramp on. The sound of a car door slamming attracted her attention, and as she lifted her head she saw Nick's car parked next to hers and Nick coming round the back of his car towards her.

'What the hell are you doing?' he rasped, and when she just stood and gaped at him he came forward impatiently. 'Come here!' he ordered. 'It's too late to help you by the look of it, but I'm damned if I'm going to stand here and get soaked.'

It galvanised her into action and she stumbled forward, searching in her shoulder-bag for the key to the cottage door and shivering more than ever. Her mind refused to take in what it saw. Nick was here, angry, impatient and getting more wet by the second.

'There's a towel in the kitchen.'

In the tiny central hall of the cottage, Victoria kicked off her wet sandals and glanced at Nick uneasily. He was staring at her in a peculiar fixed manner, inspecting her, and when she said nothing, he snapped out, 'Why didn't you take the car?'

Victoria took off her bedraggled hat and dropped it beside her sandals, using the moment and the action to avoid looking at him.

'It was too hot. I've been almost living in the car for the past few days. I fancied a walk and there was no sign of this rain then.' She looked up at him and found his eyes running over her in a wryly amused way, his previous tension gone.

'At least you're different,' he pointed out wryly. 'I've never seen you looking like this before.'

She believed him. She knew exactly what a spectacle she presented, with her dress clinging around her and her hair plastered to her head in the shape of the hat.

'I'll get changed,' she muttered, making for the stairs. 'If you hang your jacket up and use the kitchen towel you'll be as good as new in a second.'

Victoria ran up the short flight of stairs, well aware of the quizzical amusement in the grey eyes that followed her flight. What was he doing here? She hadn't felt quite able to ask as yet because she had been so uncomfortably embarrassed by her own appearance. She looked like a wet rat and it was not at all how she had wanted to look when she next saw him.

There wasn't a lot she could do about it in a few minutes, so she had a quick rub-down with a towel and pulled on thin trousers and a T-shirt. Her hair was wild, standing round her head like a golden shower of light, utterly unruly, and the application of a brush just seemed to make it worse.

What did it matter? Nick hadn't come for a friendly visit. He never did. His mission here could only be to force her to do something she didn't want to do at all, like go back at once. Victoria frowned and went down to confront him with a little more energy than she had shown when he had arrived. She was not going to let him know how she felt about him.

'So what do you want?'

He had draped his jacket over a chair and was standing rubbing his hair as she came into the sitting room.

'You're not a very sociable person, are you?' he enquired lazily, his eyes skimming over her again.

'I'm a very suspicious person,' she snapped, collecting the damp towel from the top of the polished table where he had dropped it with a cavalier disregard for the shining wood. 'When the unexpected happens, I view it with mistrust and wariness.' Victoria marched into the kitchen and put the towel to dry before turning on him again and eying him firmly through the open doorway. 'So what do you want and why have you come?'

'At this moment, I want a cup of tea,' Nick informed her blandly. 'I came to see you, obviously.'

'Why? Why? Why?' Victoria shouted. 'I'm nothing to do with you. I've come here to do a job and then get a little peace. You're too busy to follow me around harassing me. You've got an enormous court case going and—'

'It's over,' he interrupted quietly, ignoring the volume of her voice.

'And?' Victoria walked slowly forward and he sat, looking up at her through narrowed eyes.

'Guilty,' he announced. 'The sentencing comes next week.' She just went on staring at him and he raised one mocking dark brow. 'You expected me to lose?'

'I never expect you to lose,' she said in a half-whisper. 'You're too perfect.'

'Don't you mean too careful?' he enquired quizzically, and Victoria found her cheeks flushing with more than temper.

'I meant invincible,' she snapped. 'The word escaped me for a minute. None of which answers my question. Why did you come here?'

'I needed a break. What better place?'

'I would have thought Paris!' Victoria flared. 'Your fiancée is there.'

'But she's hiding,' he murmured sardonically. 'I may well have led the Press to her.'

'And what about leading them to me? Don't I count?' Victoria asked angrily.

'With you I am very, very careful. Nobody knows

where I am at all.' He suddenly stood and towered over her. 'Who knows you're here?' he rapped out with a startling change from murmured derision to sharp query.

'Muriel, Frank and Tony,' Victoria said, much of the fight dying out of her now that he was on his feet and back to normal. 'And there's Craig, of course.'

'Hmm, there's Craig, as you so rightly say.' He was watching her steadily and she took the chance to set him right yet again.

'He's married and he's my boss. I've told you that before!'

'And he's much too ready with information,' Nick muttered, turning away thoughtfully. 'He's also stupid, sending you here to this isolated cottage. I suppose it's cheaper than booking you into some large hotel,' he added astutely.

'I wanted peace and quiet,' Victoria informed him sharply. 'I wanted a rest. I was getting peace and quiet until you came.' Just because she thought Craig had been over-frugal there was no need to confirm Nick's suspicions.

'Make some tea and we'll be back to peace,' he advised, and Victoria was only too glad to turn back to the kitchen.

'When are you leaving?' she asked as the thought occurred to her that it would soon be getting late.

'Tomorrow.' He dropped back to the settee and stretched tiredly. 'I could do with a rest too.'

'Er—where are you staying?' she asked uneasily, and to her consternation he grinned up at her wickedly.

'Here with you. Where else?'

'You—you're engaged!' Victoria stammered, suddenly finding that her legs were shaking.

'Only temporarily. But I haven't forgotten,' Nick said quietly. 'I'll sleep here on the settee.'

'You're too tall.' Victoria looked at him wildly and he nodded.

'I worked that out for myself. I propose to take the cushions from the settee and the chairs and make a comfortable bed on the floor—good for the back. All I need is a spare blanket and the problem is solved.'

'What—what about your things?' Victoria asked desperately. 'Your shaving kit and pyjamas and...and...'

'I always have an electric razor in the car for emergencies. As to pyjamas, I've almost forgotten what they are. Can you think of anything else?'

He raised his dark brows and looked at her with taunting eyes that began to inspect her from head to foot. They rested on her breasts and she suddenly became aware that she had simply pulled on a T-shirt with no thought at all about a bra. His eyes were doing strange things to her and she felt her breasts tighten and surge against the soft material of the T-shirt.

'You can't stay here!' Victoria shouted, her face now bright with shock and embarrassment. She hadn't given any thought to Nick taking this attitude, and there was a small devil of excitement inside her that drove her to storming wildly just to stop its activities. And what had he meant about his engagement? What did a temporary engagement mean?

'Of course I can,' he said softly. 'You can sleep in safety with your knight guarding the foot of the stairs. Isn't that how it should be? Shall we have that tea now and then we can eat.'

'I won't feed you,' Victoria stated in a mad rush of panic.

'Just present the food,' he murmured. 'I can feed myself. I've been doing it for years.'

'I was going to have ham and eggs. It's not cordon bleu.'

'I'm quite simple at heart,' he said gently. 'Please can

we just have the tea and then eat? I've had a long drive
and then quite a fright when I found you not here and
the car standing there empty.'

'I was all right.'

'Yes,' he agreed quietly, looking at the window where
the rain was still streaming down the panes. 'You were
all right. Maybe this is the best place for you after all.'

Well away from him? Out of his hair? Victoria turned
to the kitchen with conflicting thoughts racing around
inside her head. Yet he had tracked her down here and
had come unannounced.

Her tight shoulders relaxed and she gave in to the
inevitable. He would always be there. He had told her
that in her flat, and the cottage was warmer because of
his arrival. She made the tea quickly and when she took
it back in she was smiling.

Nick looked up, his glance flicking over her face, but
he said nothing at all. He simply nodded his thanks and
looked at her with smiling grey eyes. It was as if no time
had passed at all and she wanted to sing. Being with
Nick was almost mystical, so right. Why hadn't she noticed that before?

Later, as she lay in bed, Victoria was still strangely
happy. They had not talked much, somehow it had not
been necessary, and when she had come to bed Nick had
still been awake, sitting reading one of the paperbacks
from the bookcase. He was good to be with, but then he
had always been good to be with—until his sudden re-
jection of her.

She didn't really care why he was here and he had
not really explained. The fact that he was in the cottage
was enough, and she knew that when he left tomorrow
she would go home too. She had wanted to get far away
from him but now she couldn't think why. Even if she
didn't see him it would be comforting to know he was
somewhere near.

The rain had stopped a while before and she lay in the darkness, listening to the steady drip of water from the eaves. It was soothing. It made her sleepy. She turned over onto her side with a sigh that was almost contentment. She had done a good job up here in Scotland, proved herself all over again. Now she could relax—and there was Nick, her lost hero, her shadowy knight.

Downstairs, Nick was prowling around the inside of the cottage, looking through the windows at the darkened sky. He had tried every door and window once already and now he found himself doing the whole thing again. Very few people knew she was here and she would probably be safe but it was so isolated.

He had been in two minds about coming to her, really scared that he would lead someone to her safe little cottage, but Parker seemed like an idiot to him. One hard glance and he had simply revealed where she was, in some detail.

Nick consoled himself that nobody knew how he felt about her. He grimaced in the lamplight. She didn't even know herself. Anyone tracking him would go for Cheryl, and Cheryl was in Paris.

He sighed and started to make up his bed. He would rather be upstairs with Victoria. She would be safe in his arms. Nobody would be able to get near her. They would have to go through him first.

He gave a soft, self-derisive laugh. She would not be safe in his arms. She hadn't been safe for years—that was why he had kept away from her. She had always shown her preference for Tony but now he was not too sure. Each time he had kissed her she had come to him as if it was the most natural thing on earth. It *was* the most natural thing. It had always been like that.

At the engagement party she had looked as if she

would collapse. Maybe he should never have insisted that she came but he had been longing to know how she felt about him. It had been cruel but he had known so much desperation that he had wanted some sign.

Well, he had got that, but not before he had been forced to go through with this thing for Cheryl. He swore under his breath. It was like dominoes—knock one over and they all went. He had got himself tangled with Cheryl because he had felt sorry for her and wanted to help. He had forced Victoria to watch his engagement because he had wanted to know how she felt about him.

Good arrangements—except that he was now in a small web of his own making and he could do little about it until Cheryl had made her own arrangements. When she was free of those ghastly parents he could tell Victoria the truth about his 'engagement'.

She would fly at him, rage at him. He grinned into the darkness. It didn't really matter. If she felt the same way about him as he did about her, she could take a club to him and he would stand there and let her.

There was Tony too, but after seeing him with the redhead at supper that night at the club, Nick was not too bothered about Tony's feelings. Tony, it appeared, was still playing the field, and Victoria hadn't even raised an eyebrow. He closed his eyes and groaned when he remembered how she had felt in his arms on the dance floor.

It would have to wait, though. There were Kenton's friends to deal with. The police were taking the threats towards himself and his family, Victoria especially, very seriously and so was he. He had seen the look in Kenton's eyes when the verdict had been announced. Nothing would keep the man out of prison now, but there were still the others.

The threat had been shouted in court and spoken aloud outside, on his phone, in those two notes pushed through his letter box. Nobody had gone so far before. The threats he had received in the past with similar cases had been so much hot air. This was different.

Victoria had to be kept safe, and maybe it had been lunacy to come here but he had had to see for himself that she was all right. Craig Parker would not be telling anyone else where she was. He had made certain of that. Crooks were not the only people who could make threats. He had used his considerable masculine dominance to assure himself that Parker would not breathe a word about Victoria.

In the dream she was running across a meadow, terrified, trying to escape the noise and the danger. There was the thunderous sound of hooves as the horses charged towards her, the clash of steel on steel as the knights fought, their shields catching the light in bright flashes. She could not see who they were. Their helmets hid their faces. But she knew that whoever won she would be in grave danger. She dared not scream in case they heard and turned their attention to her, but one mighty crash drew sound from her throat, woke her and still the fear held her fast.

The storm she had subconsciously feared since she had come to Scotland was raging around the hills and darting down to the cottage with vivid flashes of lightning and vicious cracks of thunder. The hot, still weather of the past days was wreaking its vengeance as she had dreaded, and this time there was no cupboard to hide in, no refuge.

Victoria lay in bed, her eyes wide with fright. She was not yet fully recovered from the dream, and almost unable to move she stared at the window, where the open curtains revealed the storm—worse in this open landscape than she had ever known before. She was like a child, helpless, and pictures she had long forgotten came crowding into her mind: her mother and father, the blackness of the night, the wet road illuminated by bright yellow flashes of light.

There was a tremendous flash of light then, a crack of thunder following it immediately, and she reached for the lamp, knocking it over in her terror. It fell to the carpet, rolled away from her grasping fingers, and the lightning came again, filling the room with an almost evil glare.

'Nick!'

She screamed his name, not really knowing if he would be there or if she had dreamed of his arrival, but almost at once she heard him racing up the stairs, tearing the door open to stand like a giant in the doorway, his face lit up by the flashing of the lightning.

'Nick!' Victoria sobbed his name, holding out her hands. Her heart was pounding with fear and she knew that only Nick could stop it.

'It's all right. I'm here.' He came across to the bed and pulled her into his arms, cradling her close as she hid her face against him. 'One day we'll conquer this,' he said against her hair. 'One day the fear will all be gone and you'll only see the splendour of it.'

'I knocked the lamp over.' She was shivering against him and he tightened his hold on her.

'I know. I heard it fall. There's no power in any case.' He reached for the lamp, moving slightly away from her and Victoria murmured in frightened protest. 'It's all right. I'll just put the lamp back.' He put it on the bed-side table and then held her again, warm and close, safely.

'I remembered,' she whispered. 'I suddenly remembered. There was a terrible storm the night my parents were killed. I'd forgotten.'

'I know. You wiped it out of your mind,' Nick said

softly. 'It's a protection mechanism but it left you with this fear. Maybe now you'll be able to face a storm.'

'Don't go!' Victoria wound her arms tightly around him and he smiled against her hair.

'I wasn't about to leave you to it right now,' he assured her, and she relaxed with a sigh of relief. It was all right if he was here.

'You're not dressed,' she pointed out vaguely, and once again she felt his laughter. His chest was bare, warm against her face, and she rubbed her cheek against it experimentally.

'I didn't actually have time to dress for the occasion,' he murmured. 'The shirt had to stay right where it was. I was already half dressed when you screamed. I knew you'd wake and be afraid.'

'You're always there.'

He didn't answer. Not that it mattered. The storm seemed to be easing and with it her fear, but she still rested against Nick in a sort of drowsy contentment. She could feel him breathing, feel the rise and fall of his chest, and she matched her breathing to his, deep and slow. It seemed to make her sink into him and her hands came to his chest, flat-palmed against his skin, the softness of her cheek rested against him.

She was almost listening to him being alive, and deep, slow warmth flooded over her, a contented excitement that turned her stomach to feathery lightness.

'Don't, Victoria!' Nick's voice was deep, admonishing and strained.

'I'm not doing anything,' she protested drowsily, hypnotised by the depth of his breathing and her own.

'You're melting into me,' he said harshly, but she wasn't worried by his tone. Even if he was angry it didn't matter, because she had never before been in this strange, heavenly world with Nick. It was something new, delicate, ethereal.

'Yes,' she agreed dreamily. 'I can hear you being alive, as if you're part of me. It's strange. I'm drifting away into warmth, safety, light. It's like that in heaven, I suppose.'

'Victoria!' He took her arms and held her away from him. She couldn't quite see his face but she knew he was angry and strained.

'Don't send me away,' she pleaded. 'I'm wonderfully happy. I've never been so happy before. I'm not afraid now.'

'There are more things to be afraid of than lightning,' he assured her in a choked voice.

'But not you.' She gave an airy little laugh, almost like music. She could see his eyes, watching her intently as his hands tightened on her arms. 'Even though you're hurting me, it doesn't matter,' she finished vaguely, moving her arms under his strong fingers.

He slackened his grip and she moved back to him instantly, listening to the pounding of his heart, searching for him in an almost mystically intimate manner. 'I need to feel close to you,' she murmured fretfully, 'like we once were.'

'Move into me then,' he said hotly against her ear, his arms wrapping tightly round her. 'It's not why I came but it's always in my mind.'

'Let me come back to you,' she begged, her lips brushing his neck, and she felt the sigh that ran right through him as his hands arched her closer.

'Come to me, Victoria,' he said softly, 'be part of me, drift into the warmth and light.'

His hand tilted her face in the darkness and his lips caught hers, consuming her, drugging her until she floated on the very edge of reality.

'Is this what you want, my princess?' he asked against her mouth. 'Is this what you're searching for?'

Her little gasp of pleasure was answer enough and he

stared down at her, frustrated that he could not see the enchantment on her face clearly.

'I want to see you,' he muttered harshly. 'I want to watch you, to remember your face as it is now. What about Tony?' he asked unevenly. 'Does he hold you too?'

'He's my friend.' Victoria looked up at him, and in the lingering flashes of lightning he saw her face, her eyes filled with shock. 'He's like a brother.'

'And me?' he insisted. 'What am I?'

'I don't know,' she said with a catch in her voice. 'You're part of me, like the air I breathe. You're everything that's gone, everything I miss, my knight, my conscience. You made me and then tossed me out.' Tears started to run down her cheeks. You belong to Cheryl—not to me.'

'Don't cry,' he said gently. 'Don't cry, my lovely Victoria. I don't belong to Cheryl. I'm only helping her out and we've got ourselves into a tangle. I'll sort it out. Come back to me. You're my princess. I've wanted you for a long time.'

CHAPTER EIGHT

NICK'S hands stroked away Victoria's nightie and tossed it aside before guiding her to him. He stroked her skin, soothing her back, and when she melted against him warmly and wound her arms around his neck, his fingers touched her breasts for the first time, lightly and gently, making her gasp with joy as heat rushed through her.

'Melt into me, sweetheart,' he whispered against her lips. 'Come back where you belong. I want you. It's like a fire inside me, and nothing else matters if you want to be part of me.'

Not a thought of Cheryl came into her mind. Tomorrow she would think of it, feel the guilt like a burden on her heart, but for now there was Nick, and she understood why she had felt differently about him for the past few weeks. Desire had blossomed without her even knowing it, and who could she possibly want but Nick? Who had there ever been but Nick?

He lowered her to the pillows and hovered over her, a dark shape above her that she strove to see more clearly. His hands shaped her face and the soft contours of her neck, coming to rest on her breasts with possessive gentleness.

'My Victoria,' he whispered. 'Always my Victoria at the back of my mind.'

He moved to shrug out of his clothes and she clutched him frantically, afraid the dream would end, but he came back to her quickly, holding her against him until their warmth mingled.

'I'm not leaving you,' he soothed. 'I've waited too

long to hold you to let you go now.' He sighed against her skin. 'I wish I could see you.'

Victoria stretched out one slender arm, finding the lamp and trying the switch, and the room was flooded with warm light. The power was back and for a second she closed her eyes against the brightness, because now she would feel shy.

'I don't want the light,' she murmured, turning her head aside, but Nick's hand turned her back to him.

'You do,' he insisted quietly, 'or later you may think this is not real. I want you to know it's real.'

When she opened her eyes he was looking down at her, smiling, the dark grey eyes wonderfully warm, with a fire behind them that made them glow. Her lips trembled and his eyes fastened on them instantly. How long had he wanted to hold her, to touch her, to kiss her? It seemed like a thousand years. His eyes returned to hers, penetrating, possessive, and soft colour flooded her cheeks at what she saw there.

'Yes,' he said softly. 'I need you. I've needed you for years.'

'You've been angry with me, pushed me away, out of your life.'

'Have I? There are a lot of things you don't know, a lot of things you've never experienced and frustration is one of them. I've wanted to pick you up and walk out of the house with you for a long time now but how could I? You would have fought me all the way.' He looked down at her, his face suddenly taut. 'Are you going to fight me now?' he asked fiercely.

It made her smile. She had brought all this on herself, and tomorrow she would know it, but for now she wanted to be here with Nick and nowhere else.

'Would it do any good if I fought you?' she asked in an unknowingly seductive voice, and his eyes flared with light as his hands tightened on her.

'No,' he said aggressively. 'I want you too damned much.' He suddenly relaxed, his lips quirking with amusement. 'You're flirting with me. Don't you know how dangerous that is? I might forget that you're just a babe in the woods.'

'I'm not!' she protested, and he moved against her, holding her close.

'Prove it, princess,' he urged softly. 'Melt back into me. I want you now, not some time later when we've had a good long talk.'

She wanted to ask him so many things. Did he love her? What about Cheryl? Why was the engagement temporary? What tangle? Would this be the one and only time when Nick belonged to her alone? But her limbs were already turning to liquid, her blood to molten gold, and she sighed against his lips as she moved closer, breathing as he breathed, drifting back into his very being.

'Victoria!' His lips were hot, burning, and his hands moved feverishly to caress her until she twisted against him in a frenzy of joy. There was a tremendous intensity between them, as if this was a destiny they had been rushing to all their lives, and every other thought left Victoria's head except the miracle of being with Nick.

'Don't leave me,' she said in a trembling voice.

'Never, sweetheart, never,' he murmured between heated kisses, and she knew deep inside that he was making a promise he might not be able to keep but it didn't seem to matter. His heart was beating strongly against hers, her skin heated by his. She was part of him, waiting for some magical moment that would seal her future for ever.

Flame shot through her as he possessed her, and her cry of shock was stifled against his mouth before the final magic came, an explosion of feeling that seemed to fling her upwards to the stars in a golden blaze of light. She clung to him with trembling hands, going where he went, following her deepest longing, and she heard him call her name as if from some far-off place.

'You belong to me.' He was whispering it against her skin, murmuring the words in her ear, kissing the burning glow of her cheeks, and it was only then that Victoria knew she was crying. But she was crying with happiness, with astounded joy, because she had not truly belonged anywhere for much of her life and now she knew she belonged here, in Nick's arms.

'Don't cry, my princess,' he begged in a broken voice, and she opened shining, tear-drenched eyes as she heard the regret.

'It's only because I'm happy,' she choked. 'I've never been so happy.'

'If I hurt you…' he began, but her fingers trailed delicately across his lips, stopping the words.

'You let me back into your life,' she whispered. 'I was lost and you found me. You always find me. I didn't even know why I was unhappy lately but now I know. It's because…'

'Don't say it, whatever it is, Victoria,' he ordered quietly. 'You're still caught up in the wonder of your first physical experience. It's easy to mistake that for permanent feelings.'

'Not for me,' she protested. 'Because it's not just that. There's so much more than—'

'Don't.' This time it was Nick's fingers that stilled her words. 'You haven't even had time to think. I never gave you time. I didn't want you to think.'

'Are you sorry?' she asked tremulously, and he moved to the side, pulling her back into his arms and settling her against him.

'No,' he confessed quietly. 'I'm not sorry. I've waited a long time for this night. I'm never sorry, Victoria. I just win. Don't you know that by now?'

'You're trying to make me hate you,' she surmised softly, and he reached out, switching off the lamp, plunging the room into darkness.

'And am I succeeding?'

'No. You could never succeed,' she answered dreamily. 'I've heard your heart beat, listened to you being alive. You're not just a dream any more.'

'Your feet are never quite on the ground, are they?' Nick growled. 'You've never been able to take care of yourself. Tomorrow we go home, and the cold light of reason will return to both of us.'

He pulled her to him almost savagely, and Victoria just nestled against him, passive and content.

'I can take care of myself,' she murmured into the darkness. 'People rely on me.'

'Heaven help them all,' he muttered, but it only made her smile.

'You don't really know me,' she said softly and he grunted impatiently, pulling her head to his shoulder.

'If I don't know you, who does? I've guided you for most of your life, watched every step you've taken, and now I know every inch of your body.'

He seemed to feel the heat that rushed into her cheeks because he reached out and stroked back her hair, tucking the wild curls behind her ear.

'Go to sleep,' he said quietly. 'Talk any more and I can't promise any sleep at all. Tomorrow we drive away from here and you go back to Clifford Court. You stay there with the family.'

'I came by train—and there's the car.'

'Is that what it is?' Nick murmured sardonically. 'I did wonder. It can be collected,' he added firmly, 'should anyone want it back.'

Victoria smiled and closed her eyes. He had obviously made his scathing assessment before she had even got back from the village. It seemed so long ago, so unreal.

'If it hadn't been for the storm…' she began, and Nick laughed harshly.

'I came to get you,' he told her. 'I've got you. Go to sleep, Victoria. I once told you that somtimes it's better not to know the truth.'

She was already drifting into sleep and she didn't answer, but his words were turning in her head. What truth? She loved him, belonged to him, and he was sorry now. Well, she had half expected that because there was Cheryl. This thing between Nick and herself had been waiting in the shadows for a long time, and now she knew it, but there was still Cheryl.

He was engaged. It was probably final anyway. In any case it was more suitable for him, for his future, for his life, which would evolve onto a much grander scale than it was even now.

'But all the same,' she whispered aloud, 'I'm not sorry. It was fate, my fate.'

Nick was asleep. She could hear his quiet, steady breathing and she moved closer, winding her arm around him, smiling again as he tightened his grip on her. Even in his sleep he was possessive.

She did not know that in the darkness Nick's eyes were open, narrowed, his brilliant mind active.

Tomorrow he would take her home and she would be safe, well away from him, because he had no intention of being anywhere near her, not until all this was over. Being close to him would be dangerous for Victoria. He was a primary target of the criminal underworld. Anyone near him would be in danger. He had to leave her until this was all over. Tony would be all too willing to chaperon the girl who had been in their lives for so long and changed them irrevocably.

He rested his head against her hair, knowing that she slept, and her name went spinning through his mind, over and over again. 'Victoria.' He said it softly into the darkness, tightening her to him even more. For the first time in his life he was afraid. He always won and this time he could not afford to lose. But there was doubt—doubt and a cold, aching dread. He had to keep her safe. She was his precious Victoria, his princess.

When Victoria awoke next morning Nick was not there, and had it not been for the imprint of his head on the pillow next to hers she would have thought it all a dream. It was no dream, though. The difference inside her told her that in any case, and she could still feel the strength of his arms around her. She wanted to hug it to herself, to stay here and never move again, but the morning had come and with it the need to confront what had happened and face the future. There was still Cheryl, whatever Nick had said, but Victoria now knew something she should have known for years. She belonged to Nick and had always belonged to him.

The sound of a car door slamming had her getting up and going to the window. Nick was just closing the door of her car, and as she watched he went to his own car and began to speak into his mobile phone. She couldn't hear what he said but from the expression on his face she imagined that someone was being told what to do in no uncertain terms. She hurried to the bathroom. Nick had looked extremely grim and she knew him well. Last night was over; now it was morning and reason had returned.

When she went downstairs he was in the small kitchen and he didn't turn round as she walked in.

'Toast?' he asked as she stood there biting her lip and wondering what to say to him.

'Yes, please. I—I would have made it.'

'I am quite capable of making toast,' he assured her briskly. 'We don't have time for anything more elaborate because we have to get off. We can stop on the way for an early lunch.'

He turned and caught the rather forlorn expression on her face and his own face darkened considerably.

'Eat, Victoria,' he ordered sharply. 'We have a long way to go and I don't want to be arriving in the middle of the night.'

She decided to take her tone from his. There was going to be no morning kiss, apparently, no tenderness, and Victoria sat demurely at the table and reached for the butter.

'I can't just walk out of here,' she announced firmly. 'It was clean and tidy when I came. I have to leave it like that. I have to put the bedding in to wash, the towels and—'

'No!' he said angrily. He sat opposite and looked at her fiercely. 'We have to get out of here as soon as possible.'

'There's nothing to stop you leaving right now,' she assured him calmly. 'I have to take the car back into Edinburgh anyway, and I have the second half of a return train ticket.'

'Second class, no doubt,' he muttered crossly. 'You're leaving with me if I have to carry you out and tie you into my car.'

'Oh, no, I'm not, Nick,' Victoria stated quietly. 'I do not simply do as I'm told. I understand that you have to leave. You're very busy. I have to stay and put things in order. If you're worried about my being here alone, I'm prepared to come home today on a later train, but that's the only concession you're about to get.'

For a moment he stared at her in annoyance, his grey eyes narrowed and penetrating, and then he shrugged and reached across for the butter.

'All right,' he conceded. 'You're now a grown up

lady. I sometimes forget. How long is it going to take you to clean the place up?'

'About an hour,' she surmised. 'Mostly it's the bedding and the kitchen.'

'Which makes it half an hour if I do half the work,' he growled. 'You do upstairs and I'll do anything that's necessary down here.'

Victoria looked at him in astonishment. He was determined that she leave with him, and in truth she wanted to. She now had no inclination to stay here and have a little holiday. She wanted to be with Nick until the very last minute because she knew that once they got back he would stay well away from her. It was all there in the tone of his voice. 'There's still the car,' she said.

'I rang the hire place and told them to collect it. The papers were still in the car and I rang from the mobile phone in mine.'

Victoria knew that. She had been watching him and she gave a resigned sigh.

'Very well,' she agreed quietly. She couldn't keep some little sadness from her voice and she knew that Nick was watching her, but she intended to put on whatever brave face she could muster. There would be no scenes, no recriminations. She had brought everything on herself, and although she still did not know exactly why Nick had come up here in the first place she was glad that he had.

As soon as she had finished her breakfast, Victoria left the table without another word and went upstairs to start her tasks. A few minutes later she heard Nick busily engaged in domestic chores. Normally it would have amused her, but right now she couldn't find much to smile about. She had lost him once and now she was about to lose him again, and he had not really said why. She knew it must be because of Cheryl.

Just over half an hour later they were ready to leave.

Nick took her things to his car and she stayed to have one last look around. It was all back to normal, but from now on things would never be normal for her.

'Let's go.' Nick came up behind her and she winced at the curt tone he used.

'I'm ready,' she said quietly. 'It looks just as it did when I came here. There's no evidence that I was ever here and not even a faint indication that you've been here either.'

She turned to leave and he was towering over her, his expression angry and frustrated.

'I don't care if there's a glowing neon sign on the roof saying that I've been here all night,' he rasped. 'If I thought for one minute that you'd insisted on cleaning the place so that no one would know...'

He grabbed her arms and jerked her forward, and Victoria looked up at him with startled eyes.

'I didn't! It was just a matter of courtesy. I would never have tried to pretend that...'

For another second he stared into her eyes, and then he caught her face in both his hands as his lips crushed hers. It was not a tender kiss. It was filled with anger, frustration and a sort of desperation that Victoria couldn't understand. He let her go when she was breathless and trembling and she said the first thing that came into her head.

'Was that my morning kiss?' Her voice was shaky and his face relaxed as his lips twisted ironically.

'Get in the car,' he ordered. 'Some things are best forgotten and this place is one of them.'

For him, perhaps. Victoria got into his car and it took all her resolve not to look back wistfully at the cottage as they drove away. Mary's Dell! It would have been better had it said Victoria's Folly. She gave a strained little laugh and Nick looked at her quickly.

'Are you all right?' he asked sharply, and she managed to nod in a casual manner.

'Perfectly. I'm just a little tired. When we get onto the motorway, I intend to sleep.'

He didn't say anything, and from her eye corners Victoria saw his handsome face darken with some emotion. It was probably annoyance and she decided to get everything over in one go.

'I'd like to be dropped at my flat,' she announced quietly, waiting for the explosion that would follow this request. She was not disappointed.

'You're going to Clifford Court!' he stated almost violently. 'No way are you staying in that flat alone. I want you where somebody can keep an eye on you and I want you well out of London.'

It was Victoria's turn to be annoyed.

'What do you mean—keep an eye on me? I'm perfectly capable of keeping an eye on myself. If you think that because of last night I'm going to throw myself down the stairs, jump under a bus, put my head in a bucket...! Anyway,' she added angrily, 'I could do any of those things just as well at Clifford Court!'

'Not with Tony following you around,' he muttered.

'I see. Now you're handing me over to Tony,' she said bitterly. 'Will you tell him that I threw myself into your arms and—?'

Nick brought the car to a screaming halt at the side of the road and turned on her furiously.

'Say one more word and you'll not need any sort of chaperon,' he grated.

'Are you miserable, Nick?' she asked, with some of her old, wondering look about her, totally ignoring his anger, and he just stared at her, the dark grey eyes deep and steady again. His glance flashed over her face, rested on the softness of her lips and then the shimmering blue of her eyes.

'If I am miserable,' he told her quietly, 'it won't be
for long. I always know where I'm going, Victoria. And
on this occasion I know where you're going too—back
to Clifford Court and Tony. Don't fight me. You'll lose.'

Didn't she always? Victoria looked away, staring at
the bright sky out of the window. It was fresh and clear
after last night's rain, the hills green and beautiful. It
was a sight she would always remember, just as she
would always remember last night with Nick.

'All right,' she agreed quietly, and she almost felt the
tension ease out of him. 'I have a job, though,' she
added. 'I can't just stay at home and—and out of your—
your life.'

'You have a job—later,' he muttered, starting the car
and moving off. 'As to staying out of my life, you can
safely leave all that part to me.'

She turned her head to one side and made a very determined effort to sleep. It would not be a good idea to
arrive home looking as if she had been up all night. She
was already sure that anyone even glancing at her would
know that she had spent the night with Nick, that she
was no longer the same.

Her heart gave an uncomfortable flip at the thought
of his lovemaking and a strange little sound escaped
from her parted lips. It was wistful, half-excited, provocative, and Nick's hands tightened on the wheel in an
uncontrolled reaction to the almost primitive murmur.

His face darkened in spite of the grip he had on himself. He could make ruthless plans but he could not stop
the quick flare of desire that rose in him, and he was
only able to relax when he was quite sure that she slept.
They would be amongst people soon, and any inclination
he felt to stop the car and pull her towards him would
be curbed by their sheer proximity to others. His jaw
tightened and he accelerated onto the motorway as it
appeared. Nothing would stop his plans, not even

Victoria—because he could not change anything now. She had to be safe, and if that meant his being away from her then that was how it would have to be.

It was late when they reached Clifford Court. The journey had been long, with quite a few stops on the way, and although Victoria had volunteered to drive Nick had insisted on staying at the wheel for the whole of the journey. Now he was exhausted, but to her dismay he refused to stay at home for the night, even though Muriel remonstrated with him.

'I have things to do,' he informed her very firmly, and that was the end of that. He left soon after bringing in Victoria's cases, and she had the problem of explaining how it was that they had arrived together.

Neither Muriel nor Frank asked. They seemed to be quite content to see Victoria home, and the rather bizarre fact that Nick had brought her and then left at once didn't seem to register very well with either of them. Tony, however, was not in any way confused and just before bedtime, he managed to get Victoria by herself.

'What happened?' he asked when she would have liked simply to disappear to bed.

'Nick just brought me home.'

'From where? As I understood it, you were in Scotland and Nick was in London. He looked wiped out, an unusual sight for him. Obviously he's been driving for a long time, and lo and behold—he carried in your luggage.'

'He collected me from Scotland,' Victoria admitted with a resigned sigh. 'I know you'll pry until you find out so I may as well tell you at once. He came up as soon as the trial was over and insisted that I come home.'

'Small wonder he's tired,' Tony murmured. 'Up and down in one day. He must have been driving all night.'

'He stayed at the cottage,' Victoria admitted as calmly as possible, turning to the door and escape.

'So that's why you both look so drawn. Want to tell your bosom pal?'

'There's nothing to tell,' Victoria choked, and Tony walked over to her, tilting her downcast face and seeing the tears.

'I've got something to show you,' he said quietly, draping his arm round her shoulders and leading her back into the room. 'I suppose you might say that I've a got promise to break.'

At least it intrigued her out of tears, and Victoria stood waiting as he found the morning paper and handed it to her.

'Front page, second item,' he said softly, and she felt shock race through her as she saw Nick's face staring up at her and the stark headline that ran beneath it. DEATH THREAT TO BARRISTER AS FRAUD TRIAL ENDS.

'Read it all,' Tony advised as she looked up at him with scared eyes. 'Nick said you were not to know but how he expected to keep it quiet is beyond me. It was splashed all over the news on TV yesterday. Better for you to know while you're here than learn it at work.'

Victoria looked back at the paper. Was this why Nick had wanted her here and not at her flat? Was this why he had told her not to go to work?

There were startling scenes in court today when a guilty verdict was brought in at one of the largest embezzlement trials in recent history. As the prisoner was led away he shouted abuse at Nick King, counsel for the prosecution, threatening to kill him before the week was out. As there has been a strong undercurrent throughout the trial of widespread criminal involvement, the police are taking the threat seriously. Mr King, who remained impassive throughout the incident, would make no comment.

'Why didn't he tell me?' Victoria whispered, looking up white-faced at Tony.

'Because he won't admit that you're grown up,' Tony muttered, taking the paper from her fingers and putting it away. 'There was no way of keeping it from Mother and Dad, and he didn't try, but you—you're different. You're not to know.'

Then why had he insisted that she come straight back from Scotland? Why had he waited for her, deposited her here? Surely he knew that Tony would tell her?

As to not admitting that she was grown up, Nick had admitted that in the most definite way.

'Why isn't he here, where we can all keep an eye on him?' she asked urgently.

'He's keeping an eye on himself,' Tony said. 'He can't just disappear, Victoria. Nick has cases piled up for his attention. I don't suppose this is the first time this has happened. He's put plenty of criminals behind bars. It's just that this time the Press were there in force because of the size of the case. It's all going to blow over. Don't worry.'

'I'm going to go and…' Victoria began, glancing at her watch, but Tony was on his feet at once.

'Oh, no, you're not!' he insisted sharply. 'I've broken one promise but the other one stays put. It's carved in stone. I'm to keep an eye on you and walk one step behind you all the time.'

'But it's Nick who's in danger,' she protested, and Tony shrugged and looked at her firmly.

'So I watch you and he keeps his wits about him just for himself. That's the agreement.'

'I didn't make any agreement,' Victoria pointed out hotly. 'If I was with him, I could watch too.'

'He's engaged, Victoria,' Tony reminded her quietly, pretending he didn't notice the tears in her eyes again.

'So what about Cheryl?' she choked. 'Who's looking

after her? If I need watching, surely she needs watching even more?'

'She's in Paris.'

'It's not the far side of the moon! And I'm a lot more capable than she is.'

'And a lot closer to Nick,' Tony said astutely. 'You've got yourself into a fine old mess, haven't you? Or, more likely, *he's* got you into it. I suppose I should rage at him and threaten to knock his head off.'

'I love him,' Victoria whispered, and Tony gave a harsh laugh as he turned away.

'I'm not altogether thick,' he grated. 'It was only a matter of time. But he's engaged and you know it—so does he.'

'Leave it, Tony,' she begged unevenly. 'You can't tell me anything I haven't told myself.'

'If I could help, I would,' he said quietly. 'I can't turn back the clock though and I suppose I would have to turn it back for quite a few years.' He gave a sigh and came to give her a hug. 'Go to bed, Victoria. You look worn out.'

She was but the thought of Nick in danger was more in her mind than sleep. How real was the threat? Was it just some angry and bitter shout from a man who had been caught? She didn't think so. She had been following the trial and so had everyone at work. The involvement of the criminal underworld was very clear to see. Would she be putting Nick in even more danger if she went to him? Did she have the right to go to him? She paced about her room and only fell asleep because she was utterly exhausted.

By the following afternoon, Victoria could not stand the uncertainty any longer. She had not reported to Craig. As far as he knew she was still in Scotland and she was glad there had been no telephone at the cottage or he would have been ringing her to check on her progress. As it was, she was home with time on her hands and Nick constantly on her mind.

There was nothing further in the paper and as the day wore on, Victoria found herself simply walking about the house. At breakfast, Frank had mentioned the scene that had taken place in court but he seemed to think it would all blow over and even Muriel was taking it lightly. Victoria could tell though, by Tony's guarded expression that he was not looking at things in the same way and she wondered if he knew more, something that he was keeping to himself.

As it was, she was alone in the house. Tony was at work of course and Muriel had gone with Frank to a flower show in a town a few miles away and finally, Victoria took her courage firmly in hand and rang Nick's flat. The phone just rang and although she knew he would be in his chambers she still had a cold creepy feeling inside at the thought of an empty flat and Nick walking back into it to face some sort of danger.

When four o'clock came round she simply couldn't stand it and went out to her car, setting off at once to drive into London. Nick would be angry, someone might see her. Apart from anything else she knew that their time together in Scotland was a secret that would never be told but she had to find out if he was all right and then she would drive home.

CHAPTER NINE

IT TOOK Victoria almost two hours to get there, because she had to go right into the city and face the rush of traffic, and it was several years since she had visited Nick's flat and she was even a little unsure of the way. It was with a feeling of relief that she finally drove down the quiet, elegant street where he lived and saw his car parked outside.

He was home. She just hoped he was safe, and she stopped her car and ran up the short flight of steps at once, ringing the bell on the outer door.

'Yes?' It was Nick's voice that came through the grid by her head and she could tell by his tone that he was both angry and stressed.

'It's Victoria,' she said, and she could hear his shocked exclamation before the sound went dead and the front door opened automatically.

'What the hell are you doing here?' Nick was already in the hall as she stepped into the place and his flat door was wide open. The sight of him, tall, safe and angry, was such a relief that for a moment she could not speak.

'I wanted to know you were all right,' she managed at last, when he simply stared at her and said nothing. 'I rang and there was no answer, and I thought about you coming back here by yourself and...'

'For God's sake!' Nick took her arm and propelled her none too gently into his flat. He slammed the door when they were inside and pushed her back against it, his hands tightly gripping her arms. 'I told you to stay at home!' he rasped angrily. 'I told Tony to watch you!'

'He can't be in two places at once,' Victoria pointed

out shakily. 'He had to go out. Muriel and Frank went out too, and I—I...'

'Looked around for mischief!' he exploded.

'I was worried about you,' she pleaded. 'I saw the paper and I began to imagine that somebody might be here when you got back.'

'You were not supposed to know anything,' he snapped, forcing her against the door in a fury. 'I told Tony...'

'He showed me the paper. I had every right to know.'

'You have no rights as far as I'm concerned,' Nick grated. 'I told you to keep away from me!'

All the life went out of Victoria. She stopped feeling the hardness of the door behind her, stopped seeing Nick's angry face. Her eyes glazed over with pain and she hung her head, saying nothing. When he tilted her chin she just looked at him blankly, registering only the cruel words, and all the rage died in him at the expression in her eyes.

'Damn you, Victoria!' he said thickly. 'How do you manage to get to me like this?'

'I'm sorry. I'll go.' Her voice sounded numb and he caught her face in his hands, the weight of his body pressing her back.

'No,' he muttered huskily. 'You can't go. It's too late. Your car is outside next to mine for all the world to see.'

'But—but Cheryl's in Paris.'

'Cheryl is safely out of the way,' he agreed unevenly, his eyes on her trembling lips. 'You're here with me, though, and you're not safe at all. It's too late. They didn't just threaten me, Victoria. They threatened to go after anyone close to me.' He gave a shaken sigh. 'In any case, you came and it was too late the moment you walked through the door because I can't let you go now. I need you.'

His lips covered hers fiercely as she started to speak

and Victoria could not move beneath the passionate on-slaught. When she gasped for breath, his tongue invaded her mouth hotly and every bone inside her seemed to melt. This was not the gentle, tender way that Nick had made love to her in the cottage. It was demanding, des-perate, fierce, and Victoria became almost fluid against him as he pursued her with relentless intensity.

She struggled to free her arms and wound them round his neck, everything forgotten in the excitement that raged through her.

'I'm always going to want you,' he breathed against her mouth. 'This is not going to go away. No matter what happens, no matter what stands between us, this is always going to be there. It's been there too long to ignore. We'll come together the moment our eyes meet.'

Victoria couldn't speak. She had come here afraid but now all she could think of was belonging to Nick again. Her fingers began to work feverishly at the buttons of his shirt, all her old shyness leaving her in the heat of the moment.

'Victoria! No, no!' he gasped, but she couldn't stop, her plaintive cry of protest uttered against his mouth. Her searching fingers touched his skin and Nick's breath sighed into hers as he gave up any attempt to stop the blaze between them.

She could feel his hands on the zip of her dress as his lips crushed hers. Her dress fell to the floor and with a groan of surrender he swung her up into his arms and put her down on the settee that stood under one window.

'Forbidden fruit,' he said with a bitter twist to his mouth, 'and you *are* forbidden right now, Victoria. You should be miles away from me but you're the sweetest fruit there is.'

He discarded his clothes and came to lie over her, not speaking, and warmly amused as he had been before.

This time there was an aching necessity about both of them and everywhere he touched her seemed to burn.

'Nick!' she pleaded, and his eyes burned down at her, light flaring in their grey depths as he came to her. He saw the colour flush into her cheeks and watched her with complete mastery as he took them both through a whirlpool of light and desire into velvet darkness. He could hear her sobbing his name and the memory of her as she used to be flashed across his mind. But now she was a woman, his woman, and whatever else happened there were these wonderful moments to remember. He would keep her safe no matter what it took.

He said nothing when it was over. His head rested heavily against her breast, his breathing unsteady, and Victoria still trembled uncontrollably, utterly lost and unable to return to reality. From anger to passion so quickly. Nick had swept her into another world and she was not quite part of the real world again yet. The real world hurt. It had hurt her often and she wanted to stay as she was for ever.

She felt him move, start to dress, but she still lay there, trembling and far away. Her eyes were closed, blue shadows on her lids, and her mouth looked almost bruised but still so tempting. There was a wild-rose flush to her cheeks, her fair hair was damp and tousled against the cushions, and the desire to crush her close, to shield her from everything was overwhelming.

'I'm sorry, Victoria,' he said unsteadily.

He stood and lifted her into his arms, holding her naked body tightly, feeling her tremble as he buried his face in her hair and stroked her back soothingly.

'I was thinking about you and you came here like the answer to a prayer. It's no excuse but I couldn't get myself together. I needed you and suddenly you were there.'

She looked up at him with wondering eyes. He looked

drawn, even more austere, his handsome face quite pale and his eyes very dark as they searched her face.

'It was me,' she began. 'I started it and…'

'You didn't,' he muttered in a shaken voice. 'Stop trying to shoulder all the guilt for everything and everybody.' His eyes roamed over her face and his lips twisted in regret. 'You look shattered. What have I done to you? You're better off a long way from me.'

'Don't,' she begged softly, and he stroked her hair back, a muscle jerking at the side of his jaw.

'You are,' he said unevenly. 'You know it now and I knew it before.' He sighed and let her go. 'Get dressed. I'll make you a drink and then we've got to talk.'

She dressed while he was in the kitchen and the telephone rang just as Nick was coming back into the room. He handed her a hot cup of tea before answering, and she saw his face tighten immediately.

'You were supposed to be looking after her!' he rasped, and Victoria concluded that Tony was at the other end of the phone. 'All right. I know,' Nick said in a more reasonable tone after a second. 'In any case, I know where Victoria is. She's here with me. You don't have to point it out! I know exactly what I am,' he added violently when Tony raised his voice. 'I can tell her myself. I'll bring her home, and perhaps you can watch her more carefully from now on!'

He slammed the phone down and Victoria hung her head again, sipping at the hot tea that was making her feel a little more in control of herself. She had brought a lot of trouble to the family and now she didn't know where it would end. Sooner or later everything would explode into the open if she didn't do something about it. She had always relied on Nick but now she knew she could not leave anything to him.

'I'll have to go,' she managed quietly, standing up

and looking round for her bag, her head still spinning. 'I know you're all right and—and I'll go.'

'If you're trying to make me feel worse about things, you're doing very well,' Nick said heavily, pacing about with his hands in his pockets. 'It's all I deserve. You came here because you were worried about me and all I could do…'

'I never tried to stop you,' Victoria said softly. 'I never tried to make you see reason.'

'Nobody has ever needed to make me see reason in my whole life,' he reminded her harshly. 'Now I just have to see you and reason has nothing to do with it, because I'm looking at what I want and I can't see beyond that. And no matter who gets hurt in the process. Nothing is going to change. I want you, end of story!'

'I'll keep away from you,' Victoria promised with tears in her voice. 'Just—just take care.'

'Look,' Nick began more quietly, 'about Cheryl…I'd better explain.'

'I don't want to know,' she cried sharply. 'You made a choice and it's nothing to do with me. Don't tell me about Cheryl!' She couldn't listen. Suddenly it hurt too much. And she grabbed at her bag, refusing to look at him.

'Victoria!' He moved towards her but she quickly stepped aside and made for the door.

'No! Cheryl is your problem, your fiancée. I'm just somebody who has always been there. I know how you've cared for me in the past. Now I'm on my own. As to making love, it—it could have been anyone. I had to start sooner or later.'

There was a terrible silence before Nick spoke.

'I'll drive you home,' he said in a stark voice. He had stopped as if he had taken a blow and Victoria was too hurt, too shaken to see how ashen his face looked.

'I can drive myself,' she choked. 'I don't need to be

followed and watched. I don't need Tony to watch me either. I'm grown up, Nick, and you know it better than anyone!'

She raced out of the flat with tears streaming down her face and he made no attempt to follow. She spun her car round in the road and drove off fast, blinded by unhappiness and eaten by jealousy. Who had she been fooling in Scotland, believing that Nick and Cheryl's relationship was only temporary? It would be for always. It had been in all the papers. She loved Nick but he simply wanted her, and all the tender, caring past was wiped away.

She drove to her flat because she couldn't face people, and after a few minutes she phoned Tony to tell him where she was.

'Don't come here, Tony,' she warned. 'I don't want to see anyone. I won't even open the door.'

'You don't understand, Vick—' Tony began, but she refused to let him continue.

'I understand,' she said quietly. 'For the first time in my life, I understand. And I'm on my own, Tony. That is something *you* must understand. Tell Muriel I had to get back to see to some work and then forget about me until I have myself together. I'll surface eventually.'

She put the phone down before he could answer, and she knew him well enough to guess that he would take a while to mull this over. It would give her time to hide away and think things through. Nothing would ever be the same again with any of them and all she could see at the moment was that it would be necessary to change her job and leave London.

If she stayed here, sooner or later she would see Nick, and if she did it would all start again because they were too enmeshed in each other's lives. They always had been, like two halves of the same whole. The dream had become reality but it was no use praying that Cheryl was not a fixture in Nick's life. Whether it was fair or not made little difference. It was how things were. Nick knew it and so did she.

On Sunday morning, Victoria cleaned her flat. She didn't want to go out in case she saw Craig because she knew he would want to talk to her for a long time and at the moment she couldn't face it. She put on jeans and a T-shirt, tied a scarf round her hair and began to work hard, cleaning things that were perfectly clean already, refusing to give her mind time to think. She moved furniture that had only recently been put in place and it was only as she found herself beginning to take down the new curtains that she came to her senses.

It was useless to go on like this. She could not spend her life wearing herself out with idiotic tasks in order to forget Nick. In any case, she couldn't forget him. She didn't want to. How to live with it was a problem she would have to solve for herself.

She was just going to clear away the brushes when somebody knocked on the door and her first thought was that it would be Tony. She stood for a moment without answering, but fairness told her that he could not simply go away. He had promised to watch her and, although she needed no watching at all, he was her friend and already at loggerheads with Nick because of her.

'Who is it?' she called as the knock came again.

'It's Cheryl. Can I come in, Victoria? I have to talk to you.'

Victoria stood and stared at the blank face of the door. Whatever else she had expected, it had not been this. She had nothing in common with Cheryl Ashton and this was going to be a painful meeting.

She opened the door reluctantly, feeling guilty and jealous all at the same time. She was the third party in a mixed-up triangle and she could scarcely believe that this was happening to her. Whatever Nick had said about the engagement being only temporary, it was a reality.

Faced with Cheryl, she didn't know what to say, but after one look at Victoria's face Cheryl came into the flat uninvited and Victoria just stood back and let her. All she could think of saying was, 'I thought you were in Paris.' Even that sounded guilty.

'I came back,' Cheryl assured her, putting her bag down and turning to face Victoria with so much confidence that Victoria could only stare. This was an entirely different Cheryl. She looked radiant too, quite beautiful.

'Can I sit down?' Cheryl sat without waiting for any reply and Victoria came slowly back into the room, closing the door behind her in a vague manner and sitting on the very edge of the facing chair.

'I was only in Paris for about an hour,' Cheryl confided with a smile. 'It was all a trick. I wanted to be back here as soon as possible.' She held up her hand and showed Victoria a new ring—a wedding ring. 'I came back to get married,' she said happily. 'I've been married for almost a week.'

Every bit of colour left Victoria's face. A week! Had Nick already been married when he came up to Scotland, when he made love to her there, and yesterday?

'You and Nick got married secretly?' she asked in a choked voice, and Cheryl leaned forward to take her hand warmly.

'Oh, no, Victoria! Not Nick. I married Terry Grant. That's what I've come to tell you. There was no question of my ever marrying Nick. The engagement was all a sham.'

Victoria just looked at her blankly. Nothing seemed to be sinking in. The only thing that seemed to register was the name Grant.

'Terry Grant,' she said vaguely. 'He—he's a pop star, a singer.'

'We had to be so careful,' Cheryl said excitedly. 'What with Terry's career and Nick's big trial the Press were everywhere—but they didn't catch us.'

'You've just ditched Nick? You've just left him and…'

'No!' Cheryl came and knelt down beside her. 'I didn't know it would hurt you, Victoria. It never even crossed my mind until the engagement party. I looked up as Nick put that ring on my finger and you looked bereft. I would have called a halt to everything then but it was too late, and Nick told me I was imagining things.'

'I don't understand. I just don't.' Victoria covered her face with her hands.

'I'll make you some tea,' Cheryl announced, standing up and making for the kitchen, and that shocked Victoria into standing too.

'You can't.'

'Of course I can. Mother hasn't left me totally drained of initiative. Stay there. You look dreadful.'

Victoria sank back to the chair, too stunned to really think. At the back of her mind she knew that Nick had allowed her to believe something that was not at all true, let her be hurt and lonely and he had done it for Cheryl.

Cheryl came back in with a cup of tea and put it into Victoria's trembling hands.

'Now listen,' she ordered seriously. 'I came today to put things right. I know you love Nick and I want to tell you how this all came about.'

'It doesn't matter,' Victoria said dully.

'Of course it matters,' Cheryl corrected sharply. 'For purely selfish reasons I have to set things right. I can't be happy knowing that I've created havoc because I was too cowardly to stand up to my mother and father. Nick was my cover. He said it didn't matter to him one way or the other, and it was only for a week anyway, but after that engagement party I knew what a sacrifice he'd made. He's crazy about you, Victoria. Give him a chance.'

'Nick?' Victoria just stared at her, but before Cheryl could say anything else there was a knock on the door.

'Oh, heavens! I hope it's not Nick,' Cheryl muttered. 'I wanted to set things right before you saw him.'

She jumped up and went to answer the door, leaving Victoria almost breathless with shock. She just didn't know where she stood now, and Cheryl's vigorous, determined attitude was making her head spin. She had walked in here and simply taken over. She was like another person entirely.

When Cheryl opened the door Victoria looked up a little fearfully, half expecting Nick now that Cheryl had mentioned it, but two complete strangers stood there, both men.

'Can I help you?' Cheryl asked brightly, and Victoria came back to reality and felt every nerve come to attention at the cold smile both of them gave.

'Oh, you've helped already,' one of them said with unpleasant amusement. 'We didn't know where you were.' He looked across at Victoria. 'We came for *her* but here you are as well, both in the bag, two birds with a single stone—the fiancée and the darling sister.'

And Victoria knew immediately who they were. She knew it was possible for people to issue orders from prison to accomplices on the outside. These were the men who were after Nick and they would use any method to get him. She jumped up but they were already pushing past Cheryl and into the flat.

'Victoria!' Cheryl called in fright, but they collected her and closed the door as Victoria dived for the kitchen and the telephone that was on the wall there.

She never made it. She'd just got through the kitchen

door when one of the men caught her and, much as she kicked out violently, she could not get free. She could see Cheryl struggling with the other man, trying to scratch him, trying to pull his hair. She gave her full marks for effort but inside she knew they would not escape.

The man lifted Victoria, holding her with one arm round her waist, and she kicked at his shins, catching him a sharp, satisfying crack.

'You little...!' He jerked hard on her hair, making tears spring to her eyes, and Victoria tried to lean forward, away from him. There was a brush on the kitchen table. If she could just reach it... 'Keep still!' He swore at her and tightened his grip painfully. 'You're not much bigger than a doll. What do you think you can do?'

'This!' Her fingers curled round the brush and Victoria didn't wait to take care. She lashed out with it, aiming behind her, not much bothering about which part she hit. He dropped her and covered his face, reeling for a minute before lunging for her again, and Victoria got one more solid blow in at him before he hit her soundly on the jaw.

Everything went hazy, the room spinning round, but just as she slid to the floor Victoria saw the door burst open and Nick was there with a man she had never seen before. There was Craig too, looking like a wild bull, and then she began to fall, feeling her head bang against the table as the man left her and tried to get away from the furious people who had burst into the room.

It's all happening here, she thought tremulously. She heard Nick call her name but she couldn't see him. Everything went black.

When she came round, Nick was crouched on the floor, cradling her in his arms, but she only came round for a second. Her head hurt badly and the room was still spinning. She could hear a lot of noise somewhere but it was not really registering.

'Keep still, darling. Keep very still,' Nick was saying when she came round again, and she wondered if he was talking to Cheryl. She wondered if he knew yet about the wedding, about that singer. She couldn't remember his name. It was Terry something.

'Is Cheryl all right?' she whispered. 'I can't see properly.'

'Don't try,' Nick said urgently. 'Just keep still, but don't you dare leave me, Victoria.'

She couldn't help it, though. She went very quiet, her eyes closed again and Nick looked up in agitation at the men in uniform who now seemed to be filling the flat.

'She's hurt!' he said violently. 'That swine hit her!'

Someone came to Victoria and Nick handed her over and then got to his feet, making for the man who had hurt her with such a savage look that one of the policemen restrained him.

'Leave it, Mr King. We'll deal with him.' He glanced at Victoria and then back at the man in handcuffs. 'Didn't get off lightly did you?' he asked drily. 'What did she use, a shovel?'

'A brush,' Cheryl said in a shaky voice. 'Victoria hit him with a brush. She wouldn't stop fighting.'

'She rarely does,' Craig put in. He was sitting on the floor too, nursing a bruised jaw but looking quite pleased with himself. 'It's always a good idea to have her on your side.'

'She loves Nick!' Cheryl said strongly. She glared at Craig as she nestled up against the very handsome man who had his arms round her.

'Doesn't everybody?' Tony asked, arriving precisely at that moment. 'What's going on here? Where's Vick?'

'She's hurt, but she'll be all right,' the policeman said.

Tony glanced with some astonishment at the men who were now in the flat. 'Just who...?' he began.

'She's mine!' Nick said sharply.

'Amen!' Tony murmured. 'And about time too. Now I can get on with my busy social life.'

'You don't seem to be worrying much about Victoria,' Nick accused him coldly, and Tony looked round the room and then back at his brother.

'There's a whole roomful of people worrying about Victoria,' he taunted. 'If you decide to let anyone near her, let me know and I'll join the queue.'

'Sorry,' Nick muttered ruefully. 'It's been one of those days. I'll tell you later.'

'The price of fame,' Tony quipped, and then his face went serious. 'How badly is she hurt?'

'He hit her,' Nick said angrily. 'I saw her fall and bang her head as I came in.'

'We'll get her along to the hospital,' the man by Victoria's side informed them. 'I think it's concussion. The fright was enough,' he added, with a hard look at the two men held by the police.

'Get them out of here,' Nick ordered through clenched teeth. 'If she comes round again I don't want her to see them.'

'Are you going with her, Mr King?' the man asked, and Nick gave him an ironic glance.

'Try and stop me,' he muttered. 'From this moment on, she doesn't leave my sight.'

Victoria came round again as she was being carried out, but everything was just a little far away and she was in no state to think clearly. At the back of her mind she knew that something important had happened before those men had burst in.

'Nick?' she whispered unevenly.

'I'm here,' the familiar deep voice assured her. 'Do you really think I would let anyone else carry you?'

'Everything is mixed up,' she sighed, resting her aching head against him, and the arms around her tightened comfortingly.

'We'll sort it all out.'

She gave a weak little smile. Nick had always sorted things out for her.

'It's a very big muddle,' she warned in a weak voice.

'I know. I produced it. Just get better, princess. We've got a lot of talking to do.'

Victoria was kept in hospital overnight. Her face was only bruised but the one thing that really worried everyone was the way her head had hit the table as she fell. It turned out to be all right, no concussion and she was settled into bed and very glad to be there. The whole thing had been a big shock and her mind was still quite vague about the things Cheryl had said.

Nick stayed with her for a long time but he was very quiet, almost withdrawn, and by the time he left Victoria had made her mind up that somehow, probably because of the dramatic events that had followed, she had not really understood Cheryl.

She was quite sure of that the next day, when the person who came to take her home was Tony.

'He's with the police,' Tony said before she could even ask about Nick. 'Don't probe about anything else because I've got my orders. Nick wants to tell you everything himself. I'm to keep out of it and this time I intend to obey like a slave. He's in one of his cold, hunting moods and no way am I about to become the prey.'

Victoria knew what he meant but it was disappointing that Nick had not come, and when Tony turned the car towards her flat instead of taking her to Clifford Court she tightened up inside.

'I want to go home,' she said unevenly. 'I don't want to be by myself.'

'Orders, Vick,' Tony grunted. 'Nick wants you to himself. He's got a lot to tell you. He's squared it all with Mother and Dad. You'll both come over later for dinner.'

'I'll be thinking about those men...'

'They're locked up,' Tony assured her. 'Nick wouldn't leave you in danger even on his worst days. Besides,' he added quietly, 'you're not the type to go around being scared. Face it like you've faced everything else.'

'I'm not as tough as you think. What have I faced?' Victoria sighed.

'A hell of a lot for a good long time. Anyway,' he confessed with one of his wide grins, 'I'm staying with you until Nick gets to your place so what's to be scared of?'

'You could have told me!' Victoria exclaimed, giving him a punch on his arm. 'You can stay when Nick comes too.'

She was worried about meeting Nick alone in case he told her something she just didn't want to know. He wouldn't say it if Tony was there. It would put off the inevitable.

'Three's a crowd,' Tony laughed. 'And who in this world would dare to crowd Nick King?'

Not Tony, she knew, and off-hand Victoria couldn't think of a single soul who could face Nick and come off lightly—not if he was in one of his cold, hunting moods. She had only seen those in court before, but now it looked as if she was about to see one close up.

'I'm a bit scared,' she murmured, half to herself, and Tony shot her a quick glance that saw everything on her face.

'Don't be,' he advised quietly. 'The villains are apprehended and you've got your man—just like in the films.'

Victoria gave him a weak, grateful smile but his words didn't really help because she just didn't know about Nick. She wouldn't know anything until he told her, and it was clear that this time she wasn't going to get even a whisper out of Tony.

There was a policeman on duty at the entrance to the block of flats and he was quite ready for them. Tony, it seemed, had already been there and the policeman knew him. It brought home again to Victoria how serious the whole affair had been. The intruders had meant to get her and Cheryl, though what their plans had been after that she couldn't hope to guess. All she could do was wait until Nick told her, and at the thought of him she felt the familiar fluttering inside that had been there for a long time—she just hadn't been able to recognise it for what it was.

Once they were inside the building Craig literally pounced on them, and looked set to accompany them to Victoria's flat.

'Mary's coming back!' he told Victoria when he had asked how she felt and shown her the bruises he wore like medals of honour. 'She came to her senses when she heard how close to danger I'd been.'

Victoria tried to murmur all the right things and Tony showed how very much like Nick he was in reality.

'Sorry,' he said firmly as they reached her own door, 'Victoria is not allowed any visitors at all.'

'Gosh! Did they say that at the hospital?' Craig asked, clearly anxious to have further bits of juicy gossip for Mary when she arrived.

'No. My brother said it,' Tony answered quietly. 'He'll be here soon, and until he arrives I'm here.'

'It seems a shame to be so unfriendly,' Victoria remonstrated mildly when they were in her flat with the door closed. 'He did throw himself into the battle willingly. You saw his bruises.'

'A tragic accident in all probability,' Tony muttered scathingly. 'According to the police it was Nick and Terry Grant who flattened the villains. Besides, Parker is married and you're Nick's girl.'

Victoria hoped so, but she wouldn't know until Nick told her.

CHAPTER TEN

VICTORIA went to rest and left Tony to himself, and it was not until some time later that Nick arrived. She had not been able to sleep but she still felt worn out by the events of the day before, and when she heard Nick's voice she felt her heart go into overdrive.

'Where is she?' They were the first words he said.

'Resting. Is everything all right?' Victoria held her breath for the answer, and she could tell from the tone of his voice that Tony was doing exactly the same thing.

'It's over. The villains were only too willing to talk. It's all further evidence. I doubt if there will be an appeal now, and even if there is, this attack on innocent people will go against them. Now we can get back to normality—if Victoria can forgive me.'

'I expect she will,' Tony muttered. 'You've given her a damned rough time, though. If she takes one of those brushes to you, don't come to me for sympathy.'

Victoria was relieved to hear them laughing but she was just a little apprehensive when she heard Tony go. She had to face Nick now, and although she had hopes they were not yet reality. There were too many questions to answer, too many things that were unexplained.

Nick would never have pretended to be engaged to Cheryl if she hadn't meant a lot to him. She got up and went into the tidy little sitting room to face him because the suspense was too much to bear; it overshadowed her fears.

Nick turned round as she walked into the room. They were alone and the air was electric between them. Both of them could feel it and for a minute he just looked at her.

'How do you feel?' he asked quietly, and Victoria managed a smile of sorts.

'Terrified' would have been a good word, but she sat down and tried to look calm.

'All right. A bit hazy, perhaps, but not tired enough to sleep.'

Even to her own ears her voice sounded remarkably matter-of-fact and she was quite surprised at her own ability to keep up a pretence. She wanted Nick to rush over to her and tell her everything without stopping, to say that things were all right. But then, he didn't look too sure of himself for once, and when he did come it was slowly, with more hesitation than she had ever seen in him.

He crouched down in front of her and took her hands in his. He didn't look up at her. His eyes were on their joined hands and Victoria's gaze rested on the dark shine of his hair as he bent over and kissed her fingers.

'I love you, princess,' he said thickly. 'If you say what you said the other day—that it could just have been anyone, that you had to make love some time—I don't know what I'll do.'

'It could never have been anyone but you,' Victoria said tremulously. 'I was hurt, jealous. I said what I thought I had to say to—to make things right for you.'

He looked up at her then, the dark grey eyes searching her face, and his hand came out to touch her cheek gently.

'Put me out of my misery,' he begged.

'I love you, Nick. I suppose I've always loved you, but I didn't know quite how much until I thought I'd lost you.' Tears came into her eyes and she blinked them away, ignoring the fact that they fell like a few drops of glistening dew to her cheeks. 'I thought I wanted to be left alone but you wouldn't leave me alone. Then, when I actually saw you getting engaged, I just wanted to die.'

'Oh, Victoria, my little love.' He came to sit beside her and took her gently into his arms. 'I've adored you for longer than I can remember, wanted you for years. I can't hold you tight because you're hurt, but I'm going to hold you tight for the rest of my life.'

He tilted her face carefully and kissed her trembling lips and it was like the first time, so stingingly sweet, so warm that she came to life under his hands. Nick gave a low groan and lifted her away from him.

'Oh, no,' he said ruefully, 'not this time. You're still shaken and bruised and, even though I'm going to have the devil of a time keeping my hands off you, I'm going to try my best. We have a lot of talking to do and after that I'm taking you home where you'll be safe and cared for. I'd rather keep you with me but there are a lot of people at Clifford Court waiting very anxiously to see your face.'

'I would have gone straight there,' Victoria said, but he shook his head and stood, then sat in another chair, facing her.

'I had to see you alone first. If you were going to tell me to get out of your life I had to have room for manoeuvre—because I wasn't going to let you go without a fight. My life depends on it.'

'And mine,' Victoria assured him softly.

He smiled across at her,

'Where shall I begin?'

'The beginning might be a good idea. For example, why did you start being cold and distant when I came back from college? And it didn't get better, it got worse.'

'You mean *I* got worse,' Nick murmured wryly. 'Oh, it's quite simple. I stopped just loving you and fell *in* love with you. I realised that you'd grown up before my eyes and I hadn't noticed. You didn't need me. I wanted you back but I wanted a whole lot more than that. I truly wanted you.'

'Why didn't you tell me?' she asked, and he laughed ruefully.

'How would you have taken it? You were just starting out with your career, just starting out with your grown up life. I had no right to tell you, no right to make you either upset or uneasy. Then there was Tony,' he added quietly. 'You were never far apart and I thought if you chose one of us it would be Tony.'

'I never even thought of it.' Victoria protested. 'Tony and I—well, we're sort of like twins.'

'Inseparable. I noticed.' Nick sighed and smiled across at her. 'Anyway, I felt I had to give you room, to keep away. After a while, though, I couldn't keep away. I wanted to see you all the time, and when we met sparks flew. I was frustrated and you were...'

'Rebellious,' Victoria said. 'I was hurt too. I didn't know why you'd stopped caring about me.'

'Caring about you! I worshipped you.'

'It didn't seem like it to me,' Victoria pointed out. 'Then there was Cheryl,' she added severely. 'Right out of the blue you brought home somebody I'd never seen before and announced that you were getting engaged.'

'A plan that almost backfired,' Nick agreed quietly.

'But what was it all about?' Victoria wanted to know. 'How can you have a big engagement party and give her a ring when it's all a sham? You must have cared about her,' she added wistfully, and it was enough to have Nick coming across to lift her into his arms and then settle her on his lap.

'This is nice,' he murmured, kissing her neck. 'You haven't been here since you were a child and crying for help.'

'About Cheryl?' Victoria insisted, and he grinned at her and stopped teasing.

'I knew Cheryl through friends,' he told her quietly. 'I went out with her a few times and got to know her fairly well. I already knew her father in a vague sort of way because he's always attempting to take somebody to court, and several of the solicitors I know have come across him and been soundly irritated. One evening I was at a very boring party and Cheryl was there with Terry Grant. They were obviously engrossed in each other. I thought no more about it until later, when I came upon Cheryl in tears and Terry ready to tear the place up. Lady Ashton had been on the phone, talked to the host and had ordered Cheryl home when she discovered that her escort was "not at all suitable".'

'Why didn't Cheryl tell her to—' Victoria began, and Nick eyed her wryly.

'Cheryl is not like you, my fiery princess. She's been dominated from birth. A suitable marriage was all that would be accepted, and after that episode Cheryl was watched like a hawk—downright medieval.'

'So you helped,' Victoria surmised.

'Why not?' he asked grimly. 'I had nothing to lose. Sooner or later my girl was going to marry my brother. I was sorry for Cheryl and miserable, ready to lash out at anyone—especially the odious Ashtons. I offered to be a cover, just to give her some room to get away. We didn't plan to actually become engaged but events rather overtook us in the form of the great organiser, Lady Ashton. I was busy, Cheryl was scared, Terry was on a tour of Europe, and before we knew it the party was planned.'

'Lady Ashton thought you were suitable?' Victoria taunted, looking up at him.

'Only just,' he admitted drily.

'Only for me,' she said firmly, wrapping her arms around his neck. 'What happened then?'

'We seemed to get into the fast lane.' He laughed.

'We were swept along and I had the daring idea that if I insisted you come to the engagement party you might just realise that you cared a little.'

'I wanted to die,' Victoria whispered, and he kissed her gently for a long time, rocking her in his arms.

'I know, sweetheart,' he murmured. 'But even then I dared not really hope. I wondered if you were just looking back at the past in a sentimental way. I had to kiss you to find out the truth, and Tony's fury at the event made me think he wanted you—just as I suspected. In any case, I had to go through with the charade. I had to wait until those two were actually married.'

'You could have told me,' Victoria pointed out severely.

'I still couldn't believe you wanted me. Things had to go a lot further.'

'Like you coming up to Scotland?'

'That was another matter,' Nick assured her. 'A much more serious matter.'

Victoria saw the laughter die out of him and she could tell by the way his hands tightened on her that he had been terribly anxious.

'It was about what was in the papers,' she said, 'about that man threatening you.'

'Not exactly. What the papers didn't know was that there were letters too, or rather notes pushed under the door at the flat. And this time they were including you in the threats.'

'So that's why you came up to Scotland?' Victoria mused. 'I couldn't quite believe it when you came.'

'Coming up there was not one of my better ideas,' Nick admitted. 'I could well have been leading them to you, but it had been so easy for me to find your exact location. Parker just babbled on, told me precisely how to find you.'

'Well, I think he's a bit scared of you.'

'Not nearly as much as he would have been if anyone else had trailed you to his primitive hideaway,' Nick growled.

'It was not so bad,' Victoria murmured, and he glanced at her with so much sensuality that her heart began to thud alarmingly.

'It turned out to be the most important place in the world, but that came later. When I arrived, and found the car just standing there and you nowhere to be seen, I think I aged quite a few years in about ten minutes.'

'It was because of the notes that you were angry when I came to your flat,' Victoria murmured. 'I thought you'd come to your senses and regretted what had happened at the cottage.'

'I was angry that you seemed to love walking into danger,' Nick admitted. 'I was furious with Tony too because he knew all about the notes and understood the danger.' He gave a rueful laugh. 'Not that rage did much to help when I felt you close to me.'

He began to brush his lips over hers, gently and slowly, and Victoria softened even more as she lay against him. In a second the tip of his tongue began to probe against her lips and she opened her mouth instantly, so warmly eager that his breath left him in a gasp of desire.

'I just can't help it when you're anywhere near me,' he muttered thickly. He set her on her feet and stood, his hands running through his thick dark hair. 'I'm taking you home right now.'

'Couldn't we...?' Victoria began wistfully, and he propelled her firmly to the bedroom.

'If we stay very much longer there's not a great deal of doubt about what we will do,' he assured her unevenly. 'Collect anything you want and let's go. Any other talking can be done at Clifford Court with everyone around us. I might just be able to keep my hands off you there.' Victoria turned to smile at him in a very provocative manner and he stepped away from her, his hands firmly in his pockets.

'Yes, you're a temptress,' he agreed softly. 'You hit the right word a good while ago. I must have made some big mistake when I was helping you to grow up. Hurry up and get your things together. My self-restraint is not what it used to be.

Victoria knew she was home when the whole family hugged her and fussed endlessly. Nick stood watching, the grey eyes back to smiling again, and Victoria looked around her as Muriel seemed to be unable to stop patting her hand and pecking at her cheek. She must have been quite mad ever to think of leaving this place. She would leave it again, though, with Nick.

Her eyes danced as she looked at him. She knew what he knew, that soon he would be ordered to tell the whole story again.

'I think you should explain all this cloak and dagger business, Nick,' Muriel finally said with a very firm look at him. 'When that man threatened you in court we thought it was just another villain making a scene. Tony tells us, though, that there were letters and phone calls. You failed to mention that. We're not exactly senile and we could have helped to protect Victoria.'

'She did a pretty good job of protecting herself,' Nick said drily, one dark brow raised as he glanced at Victoria's laughing face. 'She's also thoroughly enjoying this. She thrives on trouble.'

'How can you say that, Nick?' Muriel asked in an outraged voice.

'With utmost certainty,' Nick assured her. 'I'll be getting her out of scrapes for the rest of my life.' He reached forward and took Victoria's hand, pulling her firmly into the shelter of his shoulder and smiling down into her glowing face. 'I'm going to marry her. You can start planning that wedding and make it fast. We're not waiting.'

'You're engaged to Cheryl Ashton!' Muriel reminded him in a horrified voice.

'Now that's a long story,' Nick admitted, giving his mother a very wry look.

Muriel sat down and motioned Frank to sit beside her.

'We have plenty of time,' she said primly. 'Begin.'

It took quite a while because they wanted to know every single detail, and Tony interrupted several times with his version of things. Victoria said nothing. She nestled happily at Nick's side as they sat on the settee together and just immersed herself in the beautiful, dark sound of his voice.

She loved him so much that it was painful, and he seemed to pick up her thoughts because after a while his hand came out to take hers, to fold her fingers in the strong warmth of his.

'What are you going to do about this engagement?' Frank asked in the end, and Nick gave one of his easy shrugs.

'What engagement? It was over almost as soon as it happened. Cheryl set off from home with me each time she went out and I brought her back later. What she did in the interim period I'm not sure, but Terry looked happy enough. The first chance she got, they were married.'

'The papers, Nick,' Muriel insisted. 'It was splashed all over the magazines when you got engaged and what are they going to say when you marry Victoria?'

'The four of us will be interviewed together,' Nick said calmly. 'It will all be mixed up with this business with the police and they'll have a nice, juicy piece to fill their gossip columns. It's obvious what they'll make of it—a nice little mystery about a maiden's honour, a bit like the books for young ladies in the days when ladies swooned. The only people who are going to be stunned and enraged are Sir Alwin and Lady Ashton, and if they hadn't been so mean and domineering none of this would have happened.'

'The poor girl,' Muriel murmured. 'All the same, Cheryl should have stood up to them.'

'She's not like Vick,' Tony interposed.

'She put up a fight at the flat when those men broke in,' Victoria said in Cheryl's defence.

'She did not select a weapon and charge,' Nick murmured drily. 'But then, she didn't need to. You were there, princess. Cheryl will always have to be looked after. *You* will always have to be watched. There's a good deal of difference in those two things.'

'I don't need to be watched,' Victoria muttered rebelliously.

'I need to watch you—a duty and a pleasure,' Nick whispered in her ear, tightening her against him.

Victoria had to go to bed early because she was tired. It irked her a bit because she liked to know what was going on and she knew perfectly well that they were all sitting talking and leaving her out of it. Muriel came to her room later and sat on the bed, beaming at her.

'If you knew how happy I am,' she confessed, 'you really would be surprised.'

'I'm happy too,' Victoria said. 'I can hardly believe how happy. I'm scared that something will happen to spoil it all.'

'It won't my dear. Nick won't let anything happen.' Muriel patted her hand and gave a great sigh of contentment. 'I always hoped, you know. Nick has been such a part of your life that I thought it would happen quite naturally. Then, quite suddenly it seemed, everyone was angry. Each time I saw you with Nick you were arguing, and I knew he was deliberately staying away.

And then there was this engagement. I couldn't quite believe it. I mean, Cheryl is nice enough, but at the side of you, dear…'

Victoria had to smile at this partisan attitude but it was wonderful to feel enclosed by the family again, and Muriel had only one further worry.

'I really must hurry with this wedding,' she murmured as she got up to leave. 'Nick wants things done so quickly. One would think that having known you so long he could be a bit more patient. Now don't get into any more fights, will you, Victoria?' she added as she got to the door. 'That bruise is still very visible. There mustn't be another for the wedding.'

Victoria lay back on the pillows and laughed quietly, trying to remember exactly when, in her whole life, she had been in a fight before. Never was the definite answer, and now, because she had attempted to fight off her attacker, she was classed as a sort of guerrilla leader. She had her suspicions about the source of this rumour. It had Tony's stamp on it for sure.

For a long time she lay awake, waiting for Nick to come, but he didn't and finally she slept, a little crease of worry on her brow. Would he now keep away from her until the wedding? She prayed he would not. He had said he needed her.

In the morning she felt better and she was downstairs early, but Nick was there before her and he stood and came to pull out her chair as she came in for her breakfast.

'Sleep well?' he asked politely as he came towards her, and she gave him a bright smile, the sort she reserved for the times when it was necessary to deviate from the truth.

'Very well, thank you.'

'I hope you're lying, princess,' he murmured, bending

over her as she sat down, 'because I slept very little. I feel decidedly ragged this morning.'

'Oh! I'm sorry,' Victoria said innocently. 'Why couldn't you sleep?'

'You know damned well why,' he growled. 'I intend to sleep soundly in future, however. After breakfast you can pack whatever you need. We're leaving.'

She didn't have time to give him more than a startled look because the others came in then, and it was only as they were speeding to London in Nick's car that she was able to come to terms with the lack of opposition that Muriel and Frank had shown when Nick had announced they would be leaving after breakfast. Normally Muriel would have fussed for a whole week.

'Where exactly are we going?' she asked after a while, when Nick said nothing and drove with a sort of grim determination that worried her more than a little.

'The flat,' he answered shortly, and Victoria's stomach turned over.

'Oh, Nick! I don't want to go there really. I know I'll feel a bit timid. The men found it so easy to get in and…'

'My flat,' he corrected. 'I want you with me and I don't want you with me in the middle of a crowd. I've done without you for years. I deserve you now. I've awarded myself the sole rights to your presence, day and night.'

'It—it seems wrong,' Victoria managed uneasily when her heart had slowed to a normal beat. 'Muriel wouldn't understand if she knew, and if we're going to pretend that I'm at my flat and you're at yours…well, it seems a bit…'

'Sneaky?' Nick asked, raising his brows and glancing at her wryly. 'Darling, for a grown up lady you're priceless. As to Mother,' he added, when Victoria's face went pink, 'she knows exactly where we're going and, having been married for a long time, I assume she understands why.'

'You told her?' Victoria asked in a shocked voice.

'I did not draw a diagram,' Nick assured her derisively. 'In any case,' he added softly, 'I won't be making love to you all the time—just most of the time.'

As they walked into Nick's flat, the phone was ringing and Nick went to answer it. She could tell from the conversation that it was strictly business—somebody wanted him to take a case—and, left to herself, Victoria looked around and then wandered down the passage and into the bedroom. She had never been in here before and the starkness of it hit her immediately...

It was furnished quite luxuriously but it was unwelcoming, cold. She stopped herself from even considering what it needed to improve it. She wouldn't dare do that, she realised. This was Nick's place and, in spite of everything, she still felt in awe of him—a feeling from childhood that would not go. She just stood there, looking a trifle forlorn, nibbling at her lip, and when she looked up Nick was watching her.

'I didn't ever *ask* you to come, did I?' he said in a strained voice. 'I just swept you up and made off with you whether you liked it or not.'

'You're the boss,' she managed brightly, but Nick did not smile, he just watched her with the same old grey-eyed intensity, reading her mind, probing deeply into everything secret about her.

'I don't want to be the boss, Victoria,' he told her quietly. 'I just want to be with you all the days of my life, to love you, care for you.' He sighed resignedly. 'If you want me to take you straight back home I will, but, darling, don't think of leaving me, don't change your mind about marrying me.'

'I was thinking,' Victoria said slowly as the tight feeling began to melt inside her, 'that this bedroom is a bit like one of your court-rooms—functional, classy and sufficiently cold-looking to keep a miscreant thoroughly subdued. I want to stay, Nick, but this bedroom and I are just not compatible.'

She saw the smile light up his face and he opened his arms for her to run into them with gladness.

'I still can't believe it,' he sighed against her hair. 'Every time a wistful look crosses your face, I think I've trapped you and I feel guilty.'

'I want to be trapped,' Victoria whispered, turning her face up to be kissed. 'When I get more used to belonging to you, I'll be just the same old pest.'

'The same adorable pest,' Nick murmured. 'And how are you going to get used to belonging to me?'

'You must be tired,' Victoria said softly. 'You should go to bed. I'll come too.'

He swung her up into his arms, looking down into her flushed face, his eyes glittering with laughter.

'Are you sure you're up to this? You only came out of hospital yesterday.'

'I'm all right,' she said demurely. 'Just a little shaken.'

'But not stirred,' Nick finished for her. 'It's all right, sweetheart, I can do that.'

Later, as they lay together in the room that Victoria was determined to change, she raised herself on one elbow and looked down at him.

'You said you went out with Cheryl a few times after you first met her,' she reminded him.

'That's true.' His eyes narrowed on her lovely face as he waited for the question she was hesitating to ask.

'You must have liked her. I mean, you've done a lot for her, so she couldn't have been a stranger—exactly.'

'I never made love to her, Victoria,' he said quietly, helping her out of her anxiety.

'She's good-looking, elegant,' Victoria offered, and he nodded, his eyes locked with the blue of hers.

'She's not you, my love,' he told her gently. 'I can't order desire to come at will. It only comes with you, *for* you. That's how it will always be. Relax with me, my princess. You've had my heart for a long time. If you left me, I'd be hard, icy and numb for the rest of my life. I need you, only you.'

'I'll always be there,' she cried, flinging her arms round him and kissing his face frantically. 'Do you feel like I feel, Nick, that we're almost one being?'

'Completely one being,' he whispered thickly.

'You've been like a dream, always there in the corner of my mind, a dream I couldn't quite see.'

'Do you see me now?' he asked gently, cupping her face in his hands.

'Oh, yes,' Victoria said through happy tears. 'I truly belong to you in every way.'

'And I to you,' Nick told her with love in his eyes.

She nestled against him, waiting for the peaceful sleep that would come with Nick by her side, with his arms around her, his head on the pillow next to hers. He had always been there, constant, faithful, safe and true, one step behind her as she grew and learned to live. And now he was real, claiming her as his own, and who else could? There was not, and never had been, anyone but Nick. He was her lover, her teacher, her friend, her shining knight—and he was real at last.

MILLS & BOON®

In Sultry New Orleans,
Passion and Scandal are...

Unmasked

Mills & Boon are delighted to bring you a star studded
line-up of three internationally renowned authors in one
compelling volume—

Janet Dailey

Elizabeth Gage

Jennifer Blake

Set in steamy, sexy New Orleans, this fabulous collection of
three contemporary love stories centres around one magical
night—the annual masked ball.

Disguised as legendary lovers, the elite of New Orleans are
seemingly having the times of their lives.
Guarded secrets remain hidden—until midnight...
when *everyone* must unmask...

Available: August 1997   Price: £4.99

JASMINE CRESSWELL

Internationally-acclaimed Bestselling Author

SECRET SINS

The rich are different—they're deadly!

Judge Victor Rodier is a powerful and
dangerous man. At the age of twenty-seven,
Jessica Marie Pazmany is confronted with
terrifying evidence that her real name is
Liliana Rodier. A threat on her life prompts
Jessica to seek an appointment with her
father—a meeting she may live to regret.

**AVAILABLE IN PAPERBACK
FROM JULY 1997**

ERICA SPINDLER

Bestselling Author of *Forbidden Fruit*

FORTUNE

BE CAREFUL WHAT YOU WISH FOR...
IT JUST MIGHT COME TRUE

Skye Dearborn's wishes seem to be coming true, but will Skye's new life prove to be all she's dreamed of—or a nightmare she can't escape?

"A high adventure of love's triumph over twisted obsession."

—*Publishers Weekly*

"Give yourself plenty of time, and enjoy!"

—*Romantic Times*

**AVAILABLE IN PAPERBACK
FROM JULY 1997**

FREE!

FOUR FREE
specially selected
Enchanted™ novels
PLUS a FREE Mystery Gift
when you return this page...

Return this coupon and we'll send you 4 Mills & Boon® Enchanted™ novels and a mystery gift absolutely FREE! We'll even pay the postage and packing for you.

We're making you this offer to introduce you to the benefits of the Reader Service™– FREE home delivery of brand-new Mills & Boon Enchanted novels, at least a month before they are available in the shops, FREE gifts and a monthly Newsletter packed with information, competitions, author profiles and lots more...

Accepting these FREE books and gift places you under no obligation to buy, you may cancel at any time, even after receiving just your free shipment. Simply complete the coupon below and send it to:

MILLS & BOON READER SERVICE, FREEPOST, CROYDON, SURREY, CR9 3WZ.

READERS IN EIRE PLEASE SEND COUPON TO PO BOX 4546, DUBLIN 24

NO STAMP NEEDED

Yes, please send me 4 free Enchanted novels and a mystery gift. I understand that unless you hear from me, I will receive 6 superb new titles every month for just £2.20* each, postage and packing free. I am under no obligation to purchase any books and I may cancel or suspend my subscription at any time, but the free books and gift will be mine to keep in any case. (I am over 18 years of age)

N7YE

Ms/Mrs/Miss/Mr_____
BLOCK CAPS PLEASE

Address_____

_____

_____ Postcode _____